Kate Wood

Sir Cyrus of Stonycleft

A novel. Vol. 1

Kate Wood

Sir Cyrus of Stonycleft
A novel. Vol. 1

ISBN/EAN: 9783337245375

Printed in Europe, USA, Canada, Australia, Japan

Cover: Foto ©Andreas Hilbeck / pixelio.de

More available books at **www.hansebooks.com**

SIR CYRUS OF STONYCLEFT.

A NOVEL.

IN THREE VOLUMES.

By MRS. WOOD,

Author of "It May be True."

VOL. I.

London:

T. CAUTLEY NEWBY, PUBLISHER,

30, WELBECK STREET, CAVENDISH SQUARE,

1867.

CONTENTS OF VOL. I.

SIR CYRUS OF STONYCLEFT.

CHAPTER I.

YEARS AGO.

FEW seeing Stonycleft for the first time, walking through its spacious park, or looking at its old Elizabethan house, with the tall stately cedars overshadowing it, but would turn away with a sigh, while the thought either expressed or uppermost in their hearts must be, that it was a pity Sir Cyrus Bedfield had no son.

It was a splendid old place! No need to ask

its age when the wind whistled through, or
gently waved, the stately branches of those
majestic cedars, or the eye rested on the time-
worn monuments of the earlier Bedfields, in the
quaint old village church, setting forth the virtues
or rare qualities of a Bridget or Alice, wives of
warriors, who died in the sixteenth century;
or earlier still of the knight, Sir Cyrus de Bedfield, famed for his chivalry and prowess in arms,
or of his three sons, who followed, and lost their
lives in their country's cause,—all but one, from
whom the present Sir Cyrus was descended.

Just sixteen years before my story opens, the
one wish, the non-fulfilment of which for ten
long years had troubled Sir Cyrus' heart, was
gratified; his wife bore him a child, a frail, puny
little thing, who, as the nurse said, had scarce
strength to draw its breath, much less battle for
its feeble existence; still it did battle for its life
nevertheless, and battled successfully, and each
day gained strength, but its poor young mother—
she was twelve years younger than Sir Cyrus—

gave up hers without a struggle, and died just ten days after its birth.

Her death was a terrible blow to her husband, who was passionately attached to her, but he was not a man to show any outward grief, or let others see the anguish that consumed him; still his wife's death crushed him utterly, and he neither sought, nor expected comfort from any one, but shunned even his sister, whom he had summoned to nurse his wife, and who now stayed on apparently mistress of the baby, if not of the mansion, her head quarters being decidedly the nursery; while his were three or four rooms in a far off wing, away from everything and everybody. Here, unseen and unheard, he gave way to his grief, or accused himself of unwittingly being the cause of his wife's death. Why had he not been content with his wife's love? Why had he craved for a child? Why had he been so mad? Remorse filled his heart when he thought, that, but for the realisation of this one wish, she might never have been lost to him, that the gratifying his insane desire had killed her, and brought him as a punishment utter despair, while as if to mock him instead of the son he had so longed for, Lady Bedfield had bequeathed him a daughter—a daughter whom even to look at caused him inexpressible anguish, reminding him so forcibly, as it did, of her he had lost.

Miss Bedfield soon found that there was little fear of her rule in the nursery being set aside by Sir Cyrus, when even to name the baby in his presence, was almost more than she dared do. Being now nearly fifty years of age and never having been brought into contact with babies, the nicety and watchful care with which the little creature was tended somewhat astonished her; while the dressing of so small an infant, struck her as something marvellous, and she generally passed her mornings in looking at it as it lay quietly asleep in her lap; as to handling it when awake, that was an exploit quite beyond her powers.

Thus it was not to be wondered that at

nurse's question of, " When is the little lamb to
be made a christian of?" she should start with
something like dismay, as she replied, "A
christian! good heavens, nurse, you don't mean
to tell me that babies are heathens!"

" Lord no, Ma'am, but it's time the parson gave
it a name of some kind or another. I can't shut
my eyes to the fact that it's as weakly a little
angel as ever drew mother's milk."

Miss Bedfield gave a deep sigh, " I hope it
will live, nurse."

" Please God it may," was the rejoinder, " but
the sooner it's named the better; leastways that's
my opinion."

And if nurse's opinion then naturally enough
it was Miss Bedfield's, who was guided entirely
by the despotic ruler Lady Bedfield had chosen,
before her death, as the future nurse for her
child. But what a difficult task the woman had
set her; and how her heart quailed at the thought
of broaching the subject to Sir Cryus, who, being
but a few years younger than herself, must be

more in the dark as to babies than she was,
while as to naming it to him—so unapproachable,
so reserved, so totally unconcerned about his
child as he appeared to be ; never inquiring as to
its welfare, never apparently listening, when
she tremblingly ventured to speak of it ; and
now to have to consult his wishes as to its christening? Still there was no getting out of it, and
bravely she set to work the next time they
chanced to be alone.

" When is baby to be christened, Sir Cyrus ?"

He made no reply save questioning her with
his eyes, while a hard look spread over each
feature of his face.

She felt sure she was giving him sharp stabs
with every word she uttered, still it must be done,
and she repeated her question.

" Do as you like about it," he replied ; " in
pleasing yourself, you please me ;" and he
walked away towards the window.

" But the name, brother,—the child's name.
Have you thought about that ?"

He did not reply for a moment, and when he did he somewhat astonished her by replying;

" Cyrus."

" Oh, brother!—you forget; it—it's a girl," she cried.

" What does that signify?" he replied. " I'll have it Cyrus."

" But the mother;—the mother's name was — was—"

He turned and faced her fiercely.

" I hate the child! God forgive me, but I hate it. It shall never bear its mother's name. Never! I forbid it."

Miss Bedfield sat down and cried with vexation. Call the child Cyrus! Could anything be more absurd or ridiculous? What would nurse say? And then to hate it, too! such a sweet, innocent little thing as it was. It was shameful! scandalous! Her brother ought to be ashamed of himself. But all this abuse did not serve to mend matters or alter the dreadful name Sir Cyrus had determined on giving his daughter, and she felt like a guilty creature when nurse asked her about the christening robe and cap. How she wished the child could go without a name, or she be miles away when it was christened ; she even began to think about packing, when an event occurred which brought affairs to a climax and upset all her plans. Early one morning Miss Bedfield was aroused from her slumbers by the sound of many feet moving quickly to and fro, the hasty opening and shutting of doors, the unmistakeable something that strikes the mind with dismay, and foretells some calamity near at hand or on the threshold.

The unusual stir after the silence and gloom that had spread through and settled on the house since Lady Bedfield's death filled her heart with fear, and hastily throwing on her dressing gown, she hurried out.

"The baby is ill!" "The baby is in a fit!" caught her ear, and hurrying on, she was in another moment bending over the nurse, who was holding the frail, gasping little creature in a warm bath. Then the doctor came; and soon,— too soon—the clergyman, and Miss Bedfield found the baptism she had so dreaded had begun, and she asked to name the child long before she could quite realize where she was, or recover from the sudden fright she had experienced.

" The name, ma'am. He wants the name, ma'am," whispered nurse.

The name? Ah, the name! How she wished the floor would open and receive her! Her thoughts were in a whirl. She tried to shut out from her mind her brother and the hated name of Cyrus, to forget the place, the time, the poor baby; but close her eyes as she would, there before her in imagination stood Mr. Blackstone's tall form, waiting for her to name the child, and no other name could she think of but the one her brother had so sternly given her only the day before.

" Shall it be Julia?" asked Mr. Blackstone presently. (Julia had been Lady Bedfield's name).

"Oh, no, no! For heaven's sake, no!" replied she; and again she strove to collect her
thoughts.

Ah! happy idea! it should be Cynthia. Were
not the two first letters the same as in her
brother's name, and hating the child as he did,
might it not be months before he found out how
she had deceived him? And then, surely he
would be satisfied with the resemblance; or, his
first poignant grief over, he would view things in
a different light and forgive her.

"Call her—call her Cynthia," said Miss Bedfield, softly, as though fearing, as she looked
round tremblingly, that her brother must hear
her, even through those thick walls.

But Mr. Blackstone, seeing her hesitation,
said quietly,

"You are aware, madam, that when once the
name is given it can never be changed or
altered."

"Thank God for it," muttered Miss Bedfield.

The baptism over, with many kindly wishes for

the baby's recovery, Mr. Blackstone rose to go. Miss Bedfield followed him to the door.

" Has Sir Cyrus,—the father—the power of altering the child's name ?" she asked.

" Certainly not," was the decided reply.

Greatly relieved, Miss Bedfield went back to nurse, who, with its foster mother, were both bewailing and lamenting the baby's new name.

" Whoever," said the former, looking daggers at the pale, shaking lady before her, " whoever heard tell of such an outlandish name, or knew any baby as lived, who was called *Sin-ther*."

But Cynthia lived, notwithstanding, and though never a strong child, yet neither Miss Bedfield nor nurse had occasion to be so anxious about her again. As to Sir Cyrus, he totally overlooked her.

CHAPTER II.

SIR CYRUS TESTS HIS DAUGHTER'S COURAGE. '

STONYCLEFT was strictly entailed on heirs male, so that in the event of Sir Cyrus dying without a son, the property passed away to his nephew, leaving behind a very small mite indeed as his daughter's portion.

Was there any possibility of Sir Cyrus marrying again?

For the first five years after his wife's death many were the surmises as to whom he would marry. This girl and that were pointed out as likely to be the chosen one, but Sir Cyrus was either blind to their smiles, or had degenerated into a piece of adamant that nothing seemed to have the power of softening. As the next five rolled on, it merged into a wonder as to whether Sir Cyrus would ever marry; and now it had become a settled thing that Sir Cyrus—*old* Sir Cyrus—at fifty-six never would marry; still the inhabitants of Broadbelt—a small town about a mile and a half from Stonycleft—sometimes made it the topic of conversation as they gathered in knots about the town on market days, or drank their ale on Saturday nights at the "Three Bells."

Cynthia, I can hardly say grew up, she was so small and diminutive of stature; such a delicate, fairy little creature, with long, fair hair, flowing in natural curls down her shoulders, while a tinge of red—the only Bedfield inheritance she could, or, apparently, would ever be able to boast of, —gleamed at times like a lightning flash through it. Her eyes were dark, soft, dreamy-looking eyes, with even now a depth of power ofttimes

shining under their long lashes, or flashing wonderfully bright, dazzling glances. She was of a
fiery temperament, easily roused to action, which
was in no degree benefited or improved by the
way Sir Cyrus had neglected her. Miss Bedfield,
whom Cynthia had learned to look upon almost
in the light of a mother, had died when she was
but six years old, since which time until she was
ten, she had been allowed to run wild over the
estate, nurse alone watching over her charge, although her control was more injurious than
otherwise, petting and humouring her when most
she required correction, until Sir Cyrus bethought
him that something beyond a servant's rule was
needed for his only child, or perhaps friends had
not been wanting to urge him to adopt more
stringent measures regarding the strange, wild
little creature they sometimes stumbled upon in
the house, or chanced to see flying through the
park with a large bloodhound as her sole companion; certain it was he looked about for a
governess for her.

One was found. One do I say? More truthfully speaking scores had come and gone since then.

The dullness of the place or its stern master had frightened away some; Cynthia's temper and wilful, not-to-be-thwarted disposition, others; the latter having been so often the one excuse for a governess resigning her post, led Sir Cyrus at length to take some notice of Cynthia, and he had her taught what he himself was so passionately fond of—riding. But she was a nervous horsewoman, and nearly fainted in her saddle the first time her father took her out; he dashing across country to see what sort of stuff she was made of; she with difficulty keeping her seat, not from any inability to ride, but simply from sheer fright and consternation at the, to her, dangerous road he had chosen.

With what contempt Sir Cyrus had sprung from his horse, lifting her from her saddle and placed her on the ground, while, "Take the horse to his stable and cut him half his corn," said he to the groom, "and fetch the carriage here, *my* carriage."

It came in less than half an hour; an open carriage with a spirited pair of bays.

Sir Cyrus took Cynthia in his strong muscular arms, lifted her from the ground, where she had been seated sobbing, poised her little light figure for a moment in the air as though testing its weight, and then placed her rather roughly on the tall cusions of the driving seat.

"Here!" exclaimed he, giving her the reins and whip; "here! drive to the devil."

She looked at him half bewildered, then her pale face flushed hotly, her eyes flashed and flamed like balls of fire. She seized the reins— she was an excellent whip, having driven ever since she was a child—she lashed the horses past him, on, on, faster and faster still; until they threw up their small heads and broke into a furious gallop and were lost to view in a cloud of dust, while her silvery, mocking laugh rang loud and clear through the air.

"Young Missus can drive, sir," cried the groom, in admiration.

" Drive !" echoed his master, as he gazed after her ; "Aye, I don't know if she'll drive to the devil as I bid her, but it looks uncommonly like it."

He mounted, and turning his horse's head in a contrary direction to the one his daughter had taken, dashed off almost as wildly, clearing a deep ditch as he started, and splashing the mud into the groom's face ; who, shading his eyes with his hand from the dazzling rays of the sun, stood and watched him.

" There he goes again !" exclaimed he, as horse and rider rose in the air over some fence or other obstacle in their path, " that's number three leap—number four—five—why, no—yes ; I'm blessed if master ain't going to make for the boundary wall !"

He ran across a field and climbing a gate stood balancing himself on one of the bars watching Sir Cyrus almost breathlessly.

Far off in the distance the wall shone bright

and clear as the sun danced and played along its
sides, while the horse once more clearing a high
hedge at a bound, again settled into its stride
across a wild looking piece of moorland.

On, on they went, or seemed to fly, nearer and
nearer they drew to the wall, which looked so
high that it scarce appeared possible any horse
could breast it; closer and closer, now they are
in its shadow, and in another second horse and
rider are in the air, then disappear and are again
seen making for the wood; they have gained it
and pass away in its gloom.

The groom descended from his post of observation and gave a sigh of relief.

" There isn't another horse as could have done
it but ' Black Bess,' and there's ne'er another
man as 'ould have tempted her to it but Sir
Cyrus. It's my belief he's a riding to the devil
if the young missus is a driving to it."

And chuckling at his own wit the man bent
his way homewards, to recount to the grooms and
stable boys the hazardous leap he had seen, which

became a matter of talk and nine days wonder, to even those reckless beings ; a broken neck being the miserable end they predicted for their rash, hot-brained master.

CHAPTER III.

DOWN BY THE RIVER.

BREAKFAST—a meal generally taken by Miss
Castle and her pupil alone—had been over an
hour and a half, and the governess seated at the
window with her work, while the clock on the
school-room mantle-piece pointed at some twenty
minutes to ten.

As the hands neared the hour, she rose, opened
the window and leant out, gazing first below,
and then gradually her eye wandered over and
about the park.

It was a most lovely summer's morning, if anything rather too sultry, with not a cloud overhead,
while the deer lazily loitered under the tall thick
trees, but beyond these there was no sign of life
near, only far off some labourers tossing about the
hay, and others carting it in a field beyond.

As the clock struck the hour, Miss Castle
counted the strokes one by one. The last rang
out, and had scarcely ceased vibrating, when far
away a youthful voice broke the silence of the
still air without, and was heard now and then
above the tinkling of the distant sheep bells.

Again the governess leant out of the window
and looked towards where the voice came from,
seemingly the Chestnut-walk.

She was not mistaken. There, under the tall
chesnuts, Cynthia's small, slender figure was
moving along swiftly, too. swiftly to suit the
stately walk of the large, noble looking dog,
dimly seen following close at her heels, while
the long blue ribbons in her hat fluttered about,
not so much with the light wind as with the

speed with which she walked. Cynthia could not walk slowly, indeed it was no walk at all, but a swift gliding over the ground, unlike any one's else's movements, and Miss Castle had no difficulty in recognising her pupil, as she sometimes emerged from the shade of the trees or again was lost in their shadow.

"Ah !" said the governess, as she drew away her tall figure from the window and closed it ; "Ah !" said she, with a smile, "I thought the bright day would tempt her. It tempts me to be lazy, to read instead of work ;" and drawing a chair opposite to where she was sitting, she placed her feet on it, and taking a book from her pocket commenced reading.

The minutes sped on. She might have been reading half-an-hour, when a light step sounded without, and a soft, sweet voice, was heard humming gently, but near at hand.

Miss Castle was too deeply absorbed in her book, to either hear or heed it, until the handle of the door turned, and Cynthia entered.

Then hurriedly the book was thrust into her pocket, and the work resumed, but not soon enough to escape Cynthia's quick eye; who, save for the scornful, derisive curl of the under lip, took no other notice of it.

"You are late, Cynthia," said Miss Castle, rising, and displacing the chairs where she had been so comfortably berthed, " I had given you up, and not feeling very well, was resting a little. The weather is so warm, it quite weakens one. I feel good for nothing."

"You look so," replied Cynthia, demurely, and not a little pertly.

" Do I? Ah! well! I dare say. Shall we begin lessons? Geography first, please,—you are so backward in that,—and then history."

But Cynthia moved away towards the piano and opened it.

" Where is that song from ' Lurline,' ' Sweet Spirit?' " said she, tossing over the music. " I have forgotten the long ' run ' at the end, and want to try it over."

"Have you returned all the way home for this?" asked Miss Castle, inadvertently.

"Yes; have you been watching me?"

"I! Miss Bedfield! How can you ask me such a question? The window of this room, when I am alone, is always kept close shut; you know I never open it, if I can help it. I am so chilly."

Cynthia walked over to the window, and flinging it wide open, looked out, as Miss Castle had done, towards the Chestnut-walk, where laid Nero awaiting his young mistress, who could only just distinguish him by straining her eyes in the direction where she knew he must be.

"See!" said she, to her governess, who still stood by the window, "Is not that Nero?" and she pointed her finger as if to guide her.

"I cannot tell," replied Miss Castle, screwing up her eyes, "I am not gifted with very good sight. It may be him, but I can very imperfectly see the trees near where he is lying. Can you see him?"

"Yes; I can see he is lying down, as I suppose your imagination has just *suggested*, since *you say* you cannot see so far.   Shall we try the song?"

"By all means," said Miss Castle, rising, and coming forward.

There was nothing in the tones or words to imply displeasure, but Cynthia knew she had succeeded in vexing her, from the resolute way in which the first notes of the accompaniment were struck; but Cynthia's voice, which was always true and sweet, was especially so to-day; she showed no signs of anger.

The song was sung through, once, twice; and the "run" mastered.

"What will you try next?" asked her governess.

"Oh, nothing else," answered Cynthia, carelessly.   "It is too hot to sing any more.   This room is stifling, with the window shut; and neither history nor geography are good for your

headache, so I shall go and stroll about with
Nero."

" But the geography—"

" I hate it, Miss Castle," interrupted Cynthia,
"there is no surer way of getting rid of me than
by threatening me with it.   And so," continued
she, spreading out her long skirts, and curtsey-
ing half mockingly, half respectfully; "just
seat yourself once more comfortably in your
sunny corner, and go on with your book.   Is it
anything very amusing ?"

" Yes, pretty well," replied Miss Castle, turning away.

When she looked round again, Cynthia was
gone.

" She is the most idle girl," said Miss Castle,
aloud, to herself; " most idle."   She pulled,
almost dragged her dress, angrily over her feet,
as they rested on a chair, working herself gradually into a rage as she did so.   " Little good-
for-nothing, disagreeable chit," continued she;

"I hope I may be able to pay her out in her own coin, some day. Ah! if—if only it could be so!"

She took out her book once more.

"Bon jour, Monsieur; bon jour encore," said she, as she opened it; "oui, mon ami; if, Sir Cyrus, if she, my pupil, only knew you as well as I do?"

She tossed over the leaves, either disinclined, or feeling too irritated to read, while she continued, talking to herself, and heaping mild anathemas on Cynthia's head, until suddenly the light figure and blue ribbons were again discernible in the distance.

"Ah! little wretch, how I hate you; how I wish I may be revenged upon you for all your exasperating insults!"

But Cynthia danced along, apparently as joyous as ever, with no thought for the angry lady she had left. Presently she struck off to the right, and danced away in the sunbeams out of sight.

"She goes that way always. I wonder where

she goes," muttered Miss Castle; "I have watched her often. Perhaps there is a secret. There may be—there must be! Stay, I will find it out."

In five minutes she was equipped in hat and shawl, and out in the park.

Avoiding the open road by the Chestnut-walk, she hurriedly skirted the side of the plantation, until she reached a stile ; this she hastily climbed, and dashed along the path.

" It will lead to the river-side," said she.

On she ran, or swiftly walked, for half a mile, and then stopped breathlessly, as she came full in sight of the river, the path she had chosen suddenly winding close past its banks. She scarcely stopped to consider, but after a quick, short glance, plunged behind some thick shrubs, drawing in her dress and tucking it behind her; then she began to breathe and look about, but only the swans, sailing about majestically, or pluming themselves on the banks, met her view.

She waited patiently ; it might be five minutes,

and then a voice, unmistakably Cynthia's, was heard not far off, filling the air with its soft music, and next Cynthia herself came in view, in the direction of the boat-house. She unmoored the boat, and calling Nero, seated herself in it, and pushing off from the shore, allowed it to drift down the stream.

Slowly the boat came along, Miss Castle craning her neck, and holding her breath to observe the better, forgetting as she did so, the long bow of scarlet ribbon round her head, which fluttering through an opening in the shrubs, drifted about here and there just as the wind pleased and listed; while, at the same moment her head coming in contact with a branch overhead, displaced one of the large knobs at the end of a gilt pin she had run through her hair. It fell on to the ground, and rolled, all bright and sparkling, towards the water's edge. Miss Castle softly reached up her hand to secure the pin, lest that also should fall out and she be discovered.

When she looked up again Cynthia had taken

an oar, and was gently propelling the boat nearer the shore.

Miss Castle's first impulse was to fly, or break through the shrubs further away; but with the gentle, crackling sound her footstep made, Cynthia stood up and clapped her hands.

" At him, Nero," she cried.

The dog, with one bound, cleared the distance between the boat and the shore, and dashed up to the spot where Miss Castle crouched, who with a loud shriek, sprang up wildly to avoid him, but he was upon her ere she gained the path. Leaping up he placed his forepaws on her shoulders and buried his teeth in her hat, and in a second she was on the ground, and rolled over on to the path with another shriek even more piercing than the first.

" Call him ! call your dog ! oh ! he will mur- der me !" screamed she, groaning and trembling with fear and affright, while the dog stood over her, with his eyes burning into hers like two hot coals.

"Is that you, Miss Castle?" called Cynthia, from the boat, "who could possibly have guessed it? Are you an Ariel? or have you possession of the seven leagued boots, and from the school-room to this is but a step? Surely it must be one or the other or you never could have reached this so quickly, when I left you so busy with your book. Ah! where is that book? I will have it," cried she, suddenly propelling the boat to the shore and stepping out. "Hold on good Nero; good dog! while I search. You have been caught trespassing, Miss Castle, and must be treated as a vagrant," and putting her hand into her gover-ness's pocket, she drew forth the book, while Miss Castle, utterly powerless to prevent her, sobbed and scolded with rage.

"A French one!" exclaimed Cynthia; "well, so much the better, I will make myself acquainted with this Monsieur whoever he is, he shall be my morning's study, my French lesson in fact; so that when I return home you shall not say that I have been idle, or wasted, or spent my time unprofitably."

And with a mocking laugh, Cynthia stepped back into the boat, and taking the oars rowed herself quickly from the spot, unheeding her governess's cries for help.

As she passed round the bend of the river, she placed a small silver whistle, hanging from her chain, to her lips, and blew a shrill note, but so softly that it scarcely echoed along the river; yet at its sound Nero released Miss Castle, and dashed away over the ground after his mistress, who, standing up in the boat, waved her hand and nodded her head mockingly, as she swept with the current out of sight.

Trembling and unsteady from the fright she had experienced, Miss Castle rose from the ground, and seating herself on the stump of a tree, strove in some measure to arrange her disordered dress, which, although spotlessly clean when she started on her unlucky expedition that morning, was now soiled, and torn in several places, while her hair had escaped from its fastenings and streamed down over her shoulders long below her waist, her face and hands being scratched and torn with the brambles and thorns through which she had half fallen, half been dragged by Nero.

"Little viper!" said she, as she brushed and rubbed off the dirt; "tormenting, spiteful little thing! malevolent little creature! I hate you! As for your dog, I will poison him for letting you take my book. Yes, he is mad, and shall die!" and she shook her fist in the direction in which Cynthia had gone.

Then she rose, and kneeling down at the water's edge, dipped her handkerchief into the stream, and was about to bathe her face with it when a heavy tread startled her. But how much more startled and dismayed was she, when on turning her head, she perceived Sir Cyrus' tall figure coming towards her—Sir Cyrus before whom it had been her sole wish, sole aim, ever since she had

c 5

been at Stonycleft, to appear in her very best colours, and now disfigured with scratches, torn dress, and disordered hair, he had come upon her unawares and surprised her thus.

"Miss Castle!" exclaimed Sir Cyrus, as though questioning her identity.

"Yes," said she, rising, "yes, Miss Castle;" and then fairly overcome with anger and mortification, she covered her face with her hands and burst into tears.

"Madam," said Sir Cyrus, amazed beyond measure at her tears, and without the slightest attempt to tranquillise her—indeed, his tone was rather one of displeasure than pity—"what has happened? Have you been hurt, or insulted, or what?"

"Both—both," sobbed she, "I have been frightened to death."

"How? In what way, and by whom?"

"It was Cynthia, Sir Cyrus, all Cynthia's fault. She never came to her lessons yesterday, to-day, nor any day in fact; but here—always here, so

I—I watched her. Oh! there could be no harm in that," continued she, catching sight of Sir Cyrus' displeased look. "Am not I her governess, and answerable for her conduct? Had I not a right to see where she went?"

"The right to inquire, certainly," replied he.

"I—I never thought of that, but stood in the bushes here, and she set that large dog on me, and he dragged me out and bit and scratched me shamefully, and—and Miss Bedfield has taken away a book, a—a book that—that she ought not to read," said she, stammering.

"I do not quite understand you," replied Sir Cyrus, "surely if the book was fit for your perusal, it was for my daughter's?"

"But I—I—, it was not a nice book. It was a French one, and they sent it from the library two days ago."

"*They* sent it?" cried Sir Cyrus, angrily "and not a nice book? *They* shall hear of it again."

"No, no, I am wrong, I am so confused, I don't know what I am saying. I chose it last time we went to Cumber, I did not know what it was, I did not indeed, and have kept it in my pocket ever since, hidden away from Cynthia; and now—now she has got it from me while the dog held me down, and I could not help myself."

" And you, Madam," said Sir Cyrus, sternly, " surely you have not read a book unfit for— for—," he hesitated.

Miss Castle threw back the long masses of her hair, and looked up beseechingly in his face.

" And if I could not resist the temptation?" said she, " am I so much to blame, when I strove to keep it from your daughter? You—you will excuse my fault and forgive me, Sir Cyrus ?"

Miss Castle was not a beautiful woman, she was not even pretty, but she was handsome. She was tall and well proportioned, though rather largely made, her hands and feet nicely shaped, but very different in size to Cynthia's little fairy looking ones. Her head was small and set on rather haughtily, while her only beauty, the only one for which women envied her, was the magnificent masses of dark hair, generally bound up loosely with a coloured ribbon, but now, as I have said, flowing carelessly over her shoulders.

As she clasped her hands, and looked up so beseechingly, so humbly at Sir Cyrus, he thought he had never seen a handsomer woman.

" Well—well, Miss Castle, my dear Madam, there is no occasion for us to make a mountain out of a molehill. Cynthia may not have read the book as yet, there has been no time. I will go and seek her and secure it." And turning upon his heel he strode away rather hastily, cutting down the weeds and nettles, along the side of the path, with his long hunting whip, without which he seldom went abroad.

" Ah !" said Miss Castle, as she smoothed and stroked the long masses of raven hair, ere she tied it up. " I am glad he has seen you in all your beauty. It was after all a fortunate thing I came out this morning. I think, too, the sight of you disarmed Sir Cyrus' anger, even she—if she shows him the book—can do me no harm now, for I have been beforehand with her. And then I think—I almost think he admired me a little, just a very little."

Miss Castle knotted the bow of ribbon, picked up her hat and walked from the spot rather haughtily. As she came in sight of the lawn, the gardener was sweeping up the new mown grass. How proudly she bent her small head as she returned his salutation.

What could she be thinking of?

CHAPTER IV.

THE ALYWINS.

BROADBELT was neither a large town nor a straggling town, but simply one long, rather wide street, stretching about half a mile in length, and composed principally of shops.

In about the centre of this long street, with, on one side, a grocer, who sold not only groceries, but haberdashery, crockery, boots and shoes, and even chairs and tables—one large kind of store in fact; and, on the other, a surgeon with a brass plate on his door, like a small hatchment, only

that it was supposed to set forth the virtues and
skill of the living, and not the glories of the dead;
dwelt Mrs. Alywin, the widow of a farmer in the
neighbourhood, who had died when her two boys
were both young. Now, however, the eldest was
three-and-twenty, and she had given, according
to her husband's wish and will, the entire management of the farm into his hands some three
years since, and with her youngest son, had taken
a small house in Broadbelt.

Although the Alywins had neither the Bedfield blood nor the Bedfield birth to boast of,
still, by a certain class, not the Bedfield one,
they were looked up to and respected; while none
of those inhabitants now living could remember
the time when the Alywins had not possession of
Friarmarsh. There were some who could recollect the small homestead before it had partly
been pulled down, rebuilt, and added to, until it
was now a large, well-looking, substantial house;
while fields, meadows, and waste land had been
purchased, improved, and drained, so that the

Friarmarsh Farm had become one of the largest for miles round, and it was said, the present owner was making as much, if not more, money than his father.

Cumber, a large city, only twelve miles from Broadbelt, and easily approachable by rail, had been Mrs. Alywin's birth-place. She had lived there all her life, until she married, and there her father, a well-to-do tradesmen, still resided.

For years it had been the sole-cherished hope of Mrs. Alwyn's heart, that one of her sons should be made a gentleman of. The elder was disposed of by his father's will ; besides, farming was his by choice, also he took to it naturally as his by right; but the younger, only too gladly and willingly, fell in with his mother's views, giving over what share he had in the farm to his brother to manage for him, while he received the profits, and worked his way up the ladder of idleness and gentility. .

Mrs. Alywin nursed and fostered her own and her son's foolish wish, sending him to a first-class

school, and afterwards to college, determining,
that what was denied him by birth, should be
his by right, if it could be purchased even by the
sacrifice of her daily comforts; or, if need be, sell-
ing out her own small dividend—exclusively her
own—in the funds.

Frederick Alywin, or Fred, as he was com-
monly called, was a fair, effeminate-looking
young man, decidedly handsome, with all his
mother's horror of work, and none of his father's
hearty will of looking the world in the face, and
making his way in it. He hated Friarmarsh,
hated the sight of the daily work, the signs of his
—to him—brother's serfdom. I doubt which
was the most pleased when he turned his back
upon it for good, the elder or the younger.

There was yet one other who was not sorry to
leave the farm, a young girl, a distant connexion
of Mrs. Alywin's, who lived with her, and who,
with the strange perversity of woman's nature,
already looked favourably on the younger son,
who, whether he cared for her or no, would never

have married her, never have allied himself to more of the Alywin blood; he looked, sought higher; hoped to find and gain it. But Percival, the elder, loved her, and, as he knew before she left Friarmarsh, loved her hopelessly. So he carried his love somewhere out of sight in the deep recesses of his heart, and showed no sign of suffering, although the day Charlotte left Friarmarsh with his mother, the sunshine seemed, somehow to him, gone from his home for ever.

Mrs. Alywin, although anxious to step into a higher grade of life than the one her husband had bequeathed her; had, nevertheless, little of the airs of fine ladyism about her. In every-day life she was a busy, bustling, active body; attending to, and superintending her household duties, sometimes secretly turning a hand at the pastry or cakes; but this latter was somewhat of a labour of love, seeing Fred was so fond of delicacies and niceties of all kinds, and she was for ever studying his comforts, or whims and fancies. "He must find everything so different at

Cambridge," being the one common excuse with
which she glossed over every fresh luxury she indulged him in.   Cambridge to her innocent, but
aspiring heart, being a pinnacle of grandeur;
almost the top step of the ladder, on which her
imagination had so long dwelt.   There her son
associated with gentlemen, some, if he were to be
believed, the aristocracy of the land, and, as she
told the rector, with matronly pride, had actually
taken off his hat to the Prince of Wales.

Mrs. Alywin was rather inclined to stoutness.
She wore little crisp curls over her forehead, and
round her rosy, good-tempered face, upon which
a smile seemed constantly beaming.   Without
being vulgar, she was not a lady-like looking
person; she had had a good education, but the
rust of common life had never been rubbed off,
and she sadly wanted its polish.   She would have
been more thought of, more noticed by the gentry
around Broadbelt, had she been contented to remain *perdue*, to wait to be courted and not
court; but she aped the grand lady, and failed

miserably, her worst days being those in which she arrayed herself in a handsome back moirée and large old-fashioned gold chain; the gold chain, like the Lord Mayor's, being worn on all state occasions, and Charlotte never saw it round her neck without a feeling of disquietude and uneasiness.

Mrs. Alywin was—the day on which I introduce her to my readers—busy as usual, with some household work, an immense pair of scissors in her hand, and a large roll of long-cloth on the floor beside her, while numerous small pieces of it lay scattered about the table, evidences of the quantity of patterns she had cut.

"There goes Percival," exclaimed she, suddenly, pointing towards the window with the scissors; "and I do think, as far as I could see as he flashed past, young Johnson with him in the dog-cart," and she looked across at Charlotte Lambert, who was seated close to the window.

"I did not observe, aunt," she replied.

"Well, I wish you had, child," said she, pet-

tishly, " but I'm pretty sure it was he, and I
think Percival might choose a better companion;
and to-day of all others, too, when that stuck-up
Mrs. Knollys is sure to come in for shopping.
To-day's Wednesday, isn't it?"

" Yes," said Fred, yawning and throwing down
his book; " To-day is Wednesday."

"Then I say again I think Percival might
have been particular for your sake—my sake—
all our sakes. Don't you think so?" asked she,
appealing to her son.

"I am never surprised at any absurdity of
Percy's," replied he. "The only aristocratic
thing about him is his name—the one you gave
him."

" Ah! I wanted sadly to christen you Sidney,
but your father, poor man, would not hear of it.
He said I'd had my way with one son, and it was
his turn to name the next. We had words about
it, for I was dreadfully vexed," and Mrs. Alywin
fitted and pinned the pattern on the long-cloth
afresh, and cut away rather hastily.

"There!" exclaimed she, presently; "there goes General Knollys' carriage and pair of bays. I declare I feel quite mad with Percival," and the scissors clipped away harder and faster than ever. "He ought to have some little consideration for us, instead of apparently not caring a brass button about us."

"Don't make use of that last expression again, mother; it savours strongly of ' shop.' "

Mrs. Alywin's face flushed. She compressed her lips tightly together for a moment, as though she wished to prevent herself from speaking; but, as the flush died away, she looked up quietly, and said,

"I hope Percival will have dropped that young man before he passes the Knollys' turn out."

"I hope he will have done no such thing," returned Fred, " for he'll only commit some greater enormity, such as driving home on the top of a load of hay, or walking behind the beasts he has

come in, most likely, to purchase this morning,"
and he laughed at his mother's horrified look.

" I do not think Percival would do that," exclaimed Charlotte.

" You always take his part," said Fred.

" Not always," she answered, quietly.

" Generally, then."

He moved away towards the table where he
had thrown his book.

" My gloves are here somewhere," he said,
tossing over the things.

" Your gloves?" answered his mother, " Charlotte had them mending this morning. Where
did you put them, Charlotte? Ah! there they
are. Are you going out, Fred?"

" Yes. Have you any commissions?"

" Which way are you going?"

" Through the town, and so on into the country. It's a capital day for a walk."

" I should say you would find it terribly hot.
But if you do go, I wish you would take Char-

lotte with you; she hardly ever gets a breath of fresh country air. You know I cannot walk any distance."

"I do not care about going out this morning, aunt, thank you. I want to finish my work."

"Nonsense, my dear, you regularly mope yourself to death. Fred will be pleased enough to chaperon you."

"Of course I shall," replied he, "only make haste and get ready."

Charlotte hesitated, then suddenly rose, put down her work, and without a word left the room.

"I wish, mother," exclaimed Fred, angrily, as the door closed, "I wish, mother, you would recollect I am no longer a boy, or in leading strings."

"I recollect it very often now, Fred," replied Mrs. Aylwin. "As to leading-strings, you cut those when—when—"

"When I went to college," interrupted he.

"No, long before that," sighed his mother.

" But if you are put out because I asked you to take Charlotte, I'm sure I am very sorry. I thought you would like to have a companion; and, poor girl,—"

" Poor girl!" again interrupted he. " What is she poor for? I am accustomed to hear you say ' my poor husband,' or ' your poor father,' but Charlotte's alive and kicking," said he, rudely. " What is she poor for?—one would think I neglected her. I am sure I am as civil as any man need be. But I don't mean to marry her, if that is what you are driving at."

" Why not?"

" Why not? What a question !" said he, indignantly. " Because—because—" he quieted suddenly—" because I've other views."

" Ah, Charlotte," said he, as she entered.

" Have I kept you very long waiting ?"

" No, you are a good girl; only five minutes or so."

They started for their walk, he not in the very best of tempers, and Charlotte scarcely talking at

all, and when she did, receiving only monosyllables, or random, short replies.

Charlotte was a quiet, lady-like looking girl.
To-day her face looked quite pretty, under her
simple straw hat and drooping white feather,
while her complexion was so delicate it almost
rivalled the snowy whiteness of her cloak.

They walked on, both ill at ease with the other,
until they reached the large timber yard, round
the corner of which a narrow road led to the
fields.

Charlotte stopped, and held out her hand to
Fred.

" Good bye," said she.

" Good bye !" he echoed, in surprise.

" Yes; I am going to the Nursery Gardens."

" Very well, why did you not say so. It is all
the same to me where I go," and he prepared to
accompany her.

" No," said Charlotte; " I shall go alone,
Fred."

"Alone! What folly; not to say anything about the rudeness in turning me off so abruptly."

"I know you do not want me this morning," and she looked at him with her soft, clear eyes. "I know you were going elsewhere when aunt asked you to walk with me."

"No such thing. I'll swear it, you foolish little thing, if you like."

"It was very good of you not to mind taking me; but—but I shall walk alone to-day."

"I swear I'll come too, Lotty."

"Then I shall return home. Good bye, Fred," said she, catching up her dress, as she crossed the dusty road.

"She is a proud little beggar," he said; "I wish she was not an Alywin," and he walked on alone, deep in thought, so deep that he never observed his brother driving towards him in his dog-cart until he pulled up his horse suddenly almost on his haunches.

"Hulloa, Fred! deep in study?"

"Ah! Percival, how are you? Been to market?"

"Yes. By-the-bye, I want you to come over to the farm to see that bit of land I'm draining for you."

"Oh, hang it! you will do it very well without me. I hate poking about the farm, and you know I am an ignoramus into the bargain. Besides, I have not time; I am 'mugging' up for my 'little go;' I hope to get through in October."

"If it's for your good I hope you may," returned his brother; "but I'm just as ignorant in those sort of things as you are in farming. Do you still like the idea of being a parson?"

"Of course. I'm as devoted to it as ever."

"Is mother at home?" asked Percival.

"Yes; and there is the devil to pay if you are going there. She is in a terrible gale with you. Better not go, old fellow, if you don't want a 'row.' Good bye."

And away went Fred, heedless of his brother's question as to what was the matter.

"By Jove!" said he, taking out his watch, "it's past twelve o'clock; there will be the devil to pay somewhere else if I don't make haste."

He walked on hurriedly for a quarter of a mile or more; then turned down a narrow lane, and at length, in somewhat of a round-about way, after vaulting over a gate, was in a remote part of Stonycleft.

CHAPTER V.

UNDER THE SHADE.

FREDERICK ALYWIN struck across an open piece of ground towards the wood. Reaching it, he avoided the narrow, solitary path, overgrown with weeds and long grass, and picked his way through the ferns and felled trees, which latter were here rather numerous. Presently he emerged into another open space as wild and uncultivated as nature could wish, and not far distant from the spot where Sir Cyrus had once taken his dangerous leap on " Black Bess." Fred passed close by the boundary wall, and in another second was climbing a hill to the left.

This hill commanded from its summit a view of the whole of Stonycleft.

The view was perfect. Mountains stretching away in the far distance, crowned with trees, spreading down their sides to the river's edge ; the foliage at this season of the year being at its thickest and best. Through a vista to the right, the house—or as much of it as could be seen for the tall trees—rose dim and grey, and nearer still fields teeming with life and activity ; for being haymaking time, waggons and horses, as well as men and women, were scattered about them. Now and then a glimpse of the river, as it flashed and sparkled in the sun, caught the eye ; while the large, broad sheet of water, close to the plantation, with its small waterfall, looking like snow, was plainly visible, with even the rustic bridge and boat-house, though the latter was but a small white speck.

Frederick Alywin's eyes lingered on the river.

He traced its windings and turnings here and there; through the bend of the valley, and, again, as it glimmered through the wood, until it flowed calmly and quietly round the hill on which he stood.

There was one small shining piece, with a dark spot on its surface, which seemed to claim his especial attention. On that small speck he riveted his eyes for at least five minutes, until it drew nearer, and grew into the shape and form of a boat; then it swept away out of sight round a woody point, but now again became visible, just turning the corner by a large willow, which dipped its graceful branches into the stream.

This time the boat was easily distinguishable, as also the small figure seated in its stern ; the face and figure scarcely yet to be made out, but guessed at by the two long ribbons streaming and quivering about in the breeze, shining gaily as the sun sometimes danced about their bright hue.

Fred hastily dashed down the hill's side, and

on through the wooded strip of land to the right, and gaining the water's edge, waited quietly the boat's arrival.

It was fully five minutes before it came in sight, drifting slowly along with the current, which here was not strong but deep, the water shining on the side on which Fred stood, like burnished steel; but on the other it glimmered darkly like a guilty thing, from under the shade cast by the high wooded mountains.

A bright flush suffused Cynthia's face, as, taking the oars, she rowed to the spot where Frederick Alywin stood, who, as he noticed her confusion, mentally resolved to hazard the die that should decide his fate and hers, for ever!

"At last!" said he, as, securing the boat to the shore, he helped her to alight.

She sprang out lightly, the weight of her small body scarce bending the boat as she placed her foot on its edge; while Nero, who hastened to follow his mistress's example, almost dipped it under water as he clambered over its side.

Although he addressed Cynthia so familiarly, Frederick neither took her hand nor seemed by his looks glad to see her, but prepared to walk by her side in moody silence, while Nero stretched his huge body at full length alongside where the boat lay moored.

" Are you vexed because I am so late?" asked Cynthia, timidly.

" Not exactly vexed, but out of patience. You are nearly half-an-hour late."

" I know I am."

The quietness with which she answered seemed to irritate him, for he replied sharply—

" And no regret for it! If you only knew, Miss Bedfield, how nearly wild you drive me sometimes. How mad with jealousy!"

" What can you have to be jealous of?" she asked.

" Did I not see that fellow Knollys riding down the town as if for a wager, and dashing through the park gates as though a thousand devils were at his heels? and this, too, almost at the very hour when you said you would meet me here."

" Did he ?" said Cynthia, simply ; " then you could not have been to your time either, since you saw him."

" Where was the use? I guessed where he was going when I saw him galloping through the town, and knew you would sit chatting with him all the morning, as it seems you have, while I have been all the while devoured with jealous thoughts."

" You have no right," replied Cynthia, haughtily, " to be jealous."

His anger and pettishness died away instantaneously, he turned his head and looked at her earnestly ; so earnestly that again the bright flush burnt her cheeks with its deep red.

" Will you give me the right, Miss Bedfield ?" he asked, softly.

" No," she replied firmly ; " No, I will never give you the right to be jealous of me. And you have no cause for it now, for I never saw Captain

Knollys. It was that tiresome Miss Castle who
kept me." And then she laughingly told the
history of that lady's misadventure; " and indeed, Mr. Alywin," said she, as she concluded,
" I don't think I can come again, or at least not
so often, because since she has begun to suspect
me she will be for ever on the watch out of spite,
if for nothing else ; and if papa were to find it
out he—he -, Oh ! I do not know what he would
say."

They had turned the bend of the river as it
wound round the hill, and were now out of sight
of the boat. Fred led her towards a large tree,
and seated her under its shade, while he threw
himself on the ground at her feet.

" And so you do not wish to see me again,
Miss Bedfield ?" he asked, somewhat sorrowfully.

" I did not say that. I merely wished to say
I thought it would be dangerous."

" Are you afraid ?"

" Afraid !" she repeated, scornfully, while her

eyes flashed indignantly; "afraid! am I not a Bedfield?"

His lip curled sarcastically.

"Ah! true. The Bedfields know no fear. I was, I confess, nearly forgetting for the moment that you were a Bedfield."

"Do you say that tauntingly?" asked Cynthia, drawing her head up proudly, as she remarked the expression that flitted over his face.

"God forbid."

They were both for a moment silent; and then,

"Would you brave no danger for my sake, Miss Bedfield?" he asked.

Cynthia did not reply, and for a while neither spoke, until Fred, half raising himself from the ground, and bending his eyes on her partially averted face, said,

"Cynthia, do you remember the day when I rescued the poor thrush from Nero's jaws? It is not so very long ago, only six months—if that. How you sobbed and cried when I took it from him. See! I have the mark of his teeth on my hand yet."

"I was but a child then. And besides, the poor bird was dead; you rescued it too late."

"You are little more than a child now; or," corrected he, seeing her offended look, "even allowing that you are, you have still the same tender heart you had then, and I am going to ask its compassion—nay more, its love. Don't look so frightened, Cynthia; that I love you, you, child or woman, must have guessed lately, though not guessed for how long. Cynthia, I had seen you many times before the day on which Nero's breach of faith brought us into contact. Often and often I had watched you until my heart was ready to worship your goodness, even as my eyes had your loveliness. How many wise resolutions that I have never had the strength of mind to keep, have I formed since then! It was but to see you to overthrow them. When I last went back to Cambridge, I determined I would never see you again, never put myself in the way

of temptation ; you know how little I have been
able to resist it, and how often since my return I
have been at your side, or always about here
watching and waiting for you. To-day I can no
longer smother my feelings, or check my words,
whether right or wrong I cannot help telling you
that I love you, Cynthia, and ask for the only
thing that can make a better man of me—your
love. Will you—do you love me, Cynthia ?"

She had no answer save the loving light in her
eyes, as he drew her unresistingly towards him,
and kissed her passionately.

" There is nothing, darling mine," said he, presently, " that I would not bear for your dear sake.
Taunts, derision, slander, disgrace, even curses of
those nearest and dearest to me. Is your love
like this, Cynthia ?   Do you love me so ?"

" I love you very dearly," she replied ; " but
as to all those dreadful things you talk of, no
one cares for me enough to put me to the test of
whether I would bear them for your sake, or
no."

"You are wrong, Cynthia. Your father, Sir Cyrus, will never *freely* give his consent to your being my wife."

"What! not when he has hated me ever since I was born? Old nurse says he has never forgotten his disappointment at my being a girl, or forgiven my being the innocent cause of poor mamma's death."

"Perhaps not. Yet from him will come all the trials you will have to bear for my sake, and reason as you will they *must*, will be many, and great. Recollect he is a Bedfield, and a proud one, even of that proud stock, and that is saying a great deal when pride is the one prominent quality besides blood your race have to boast of; and yet you think, poor little one, he will willingly consent to give you to an Alwyn? one of a stock," said Fred, bitterly, "who have been *kicked* out of Stonycleft."

"Yes; but nurse says it was done in a fit of passion, and because one of the Alwyns insulted my grandfather." •

" True, Cynthia. In much the same way in which I am insulting the present one, by presuming to love his daughter. He, my father, went boldly and confronted the lion in his den, and was kicked out for his presumption. I, his son, will be wiser, Cynthia; I swear I will never brook an indignity of that sort; I will never ask your father to sanction our love. Never! If you are to be mine, it must be without his knowledge."

" Oh! no, no; not that way," replied Cynthia.

" It can be no other. Your father has never cared for you. Neither will he much care whom you marry; still, as a Bedfield he will not, cannot countenance an alliance with one whom *his* father did not think fit for his daughter; but he will only too gladly give in and forgive us, when once the thing is irrevocable. I do not ask you to be mine now at once, Cynthia. I must wait until I am in orders, and then say, dearest, that you will come to me and be my wife in spite of all and everything, no matter what happens."

"I will always ask my father first," said Cynthia, clasping her hands. " I will pray him to listen to me, and not break my heart."

"It will be useless, Cynthia; he will *never* willingly grant it. But you will not take your love from me when I only live for that. If you do, I care little what becomes of me. I will go abroad, emigrate to Australia ; but forget you? Never! and you, Cynthia, you will never be untrue to me, darling?"

" Untrue! no. No Bedfield ever went back from their word. I will love you always—that is, as long as you desire my love. My poor aunt never married, she loved your father faithfully to the last, if not in her heart, in her memory, although he forsook his early love. Perhaps it will be so now," said she, mournfully.

" Never! Cynthia. I swear I will love you as long as my heart beats," and once more he drew her near him, and kissed her passionately.

And now we will leave them, and turn to Sir Cyrus, whom we left pursuing his way along the river side, in search of his daughter and the book.

Sir Cyrus walked hastily; but soon slackened his speed, expecting at every turn of the river to see Cynthia. But the boat had had too long a start, and besides, just here the current was strong and ran along much faster than he leisurely walked.

After a little while his monotonous walk set his thoughts wandering, and they wandered, somehow, towards Miss Castle and the raven masses of hair he had seen falling like a thick veil over her shoulders, down to the ground on either side as she knelt.

"Lovely hair," he murmured; "lovely! I never saw such a profusion, or such a length. I wonder if she heard my step along the walk and let it down on purpose, like that Lady Festing, who pretended she had sprained her ancle so that I might admire her foot. Well, I did admire it; nay more, I kissed it. But I never thought of kissing her," and then he laughed as though some amusing reminiscence had suddenly come across his mind. Next he considered how long Miss Castle had been at Stonycleft, and counted the months one by one on his fingers. " More than ten," said he ; "a longer time than any of those ladies who preceded her. So she must have a pretty good temper, otherwise like the rest she would have left long ago." But it never occurred to him, that some hidden motive or purpose, besides his daughter's education, lurked at the bottom of Miss Castle's forbearance.

Just as his thoughts were settling the question of Miss Castle's temper, he suddenly saw through a slight break in the bushes, the boat, not a hundred yards distant. A glance told him it was empty. A second that Nero lay stretched beside it.

Sir Cyrus halted while his eyes instantly searched the banks as far as the river went, but his view was soon intercepted by the hill round which it disappeared.

His suspicions were aroused. His determination taken in a moment. Cautiously he advanced round the corner, but Nero saw him, and with a low growl sprung to his feet; but at the same moment a soft whistle from Sir Cyrus, and the dog suddenly turned and lay down again.

Sir Cyrus walked on seeing nothing further to bar his progress, and reaching the spot where Nero lay, he took from his pocket a piece of string. Doubling and knotting it, he tied the dog by his collar to the chain of the boat, and stood and took a cursory survey of the ground. Presently he went away up the narrow strip of ground, down which Frederick Alywin had so impetuously dashed. Reaching the top he again stood and reconnoitred, before he made his way round the base of the hill, towards where the river had from below flowed away out of his sight.

Advancing to the edge of the cliff, he looked below. The next moment his face flushed and burnt as hotly as Cynthia's had done only a short while ago.

Fred had seated Cynthia on that side of the tree nearest the cliff, so that its branches hardly afforded a screen from Sir Cyrus' gaze. With what a deadly look of rage his eyes glittered as he stood there looking at them. Frederick Alywin's arm encircling his daughter's waist, while she leant her head lovingly against his shoulder, a small streak of light coming across her fair hair and lighting it up like a golden shower.

Sir Cyrus took it all in at a glance, and then with a smothered oath, strode away, clenching his long riding whip firmly and tightly in his strong hand, while his face was as pale and dark as night.

On through the wooded strip, down again to the boat, where still lay Nero, who this time unwarned by the well known sound of his master's whistle, bayed out furiously at the sound of approaching footsteps, then crouched down humbly as Sir Cyrus passed him swiftly, and turning the corner stood before the affrighted Cynthia and her lover, just as they had evidently been aroused by the sound of Nero's voice.

"Sir Cyrus! papa!" exclaimed Cynthia, tremblingly, then catching sight of his pale, stern, angry face, uplifted arm and hand, from which the long end of the whip fell, she darted forward, and terrified, tried to cling round his waist, But he threw her from him as though she had been a feather. She fell striking her forehead against a stone ; but Sir Cyrus never stayed his steps, but strode fiercely on to where Frederick Alywin stood, as it were, at bay. Grasping him in his powerful hand, the whip descended mercilessly and savagely, while oaths and execrations fell thick and fast from the infuriated Sir Cyrus' lips. Then he flung him from him.

"Away, vile hound! begone!" he shouted, fiercely, "miserable cur of a cowardly father, and never dare touch a Bedfield again, or come within speech of my daughter, or I'll give you some further proofs of a Bedfield's rage and strength."

And turning to Cynthia, who with her face buried in her hand sat sobbing on the ground, he bade her, sharply, " get up and begone."

But Cynthia never stirred.

" Get up !" he cried, angrily, " get up and go home," and at the same time he seized her roughly by the arm.

Cynthia started up and shook off his hand as though it had stung her, her face more set and determined ; more pale than his . own, except where the blood, from the blow of the stone, stained her white forehead.

" Yes !" she said, " yes, I will get up ! I will begone ! but not through fear. Oh, not through fear !" and again the same wild light, he had once seen, when he put the reins into her hands and bade her drive to the devil, played in her eyes, " you have treated me—him harshly, and unjustifiably, and you will live to regret it ! to hate it ! even as you hate me !" So saying, she fled rapidly from the spot, and before Sir Cyrus could reach the boat, she was seated in it and away in the middle of the stream, laughing defiantly at him, as he strode after her along the bank.

"Regret it!" said Frederick Alywin, as some time after he with pain and difficulty arose from the ground; "Regret it!" said he, again, bitterly. "Aye, and if he lives I'll make him curse the remembrance of it, too."

CHAPTER VI.

BEARDING THE LION.

THAT evening Sir Cyrus sent for his daughter into his study or smoking room. She was a long time in coming, so long that he began to think she did not intend answering his summons; but she came at last, looking very different from what he expected.

He thought to have found her still angry and rebellious; still determined on thwarting his will; but her appearance startled if not shocked him.

E 2

Her face was as white as death, save where a bright red spot burnt in either cheek, while her right temple looked swelled and painful from the recent injury it had received. Her eyes had a strange unnatural light, the lids weighed down heavily from recent weeping, the long lashes quite shading her cheek. She might still be angry and rebellious, but there was no outward sign of it; pain and suffering was all Sir Cyrus could detect during the stern, searching glance he bent on her as she entered the room.

"Sit down, child. Why did you not come sooner?. You have kept me waiting a long time." His words were harsh, but a touch of kindness lurked in the tone of his voice.

"Nurse was bathing my forehead."

"Is it very painful?"

"Nothing but what I can bear."

Was this said reproachfully and accusingly, as though she thought him capable of having purposely hurt her? Sir Cyrus thought so.

"It was purely accidental. I never intended

it," he put the words almost as a question; but
Cynthia paid no heed to them.

He waited as though expecting an answer, and
then said testily—

"You cannot think I intended the blow,
child?"

She was still silent, and Sir Cyrus grew exasperated. "What!" exclaimed he, angrily, "you
accuse me of having hurt you intentionally? Me,
your father. How dare you!" and he brought
his clenched fist down violently on the table.

"You startle and frighten me," said Cynthia,
"I do not know what you want me to say."

"Nothing," he replied moodily; "let the
stain rest on me since it so pleases you. I will
not urge an answer. But as to that—what I
found out this morning. How long has it been
going on? How long have you known that—
fellow?" asked Sir Cyrus, hesitating, and then
substituting the latter word for the much harsher
and stronger expression that first rose to his
lips.

"Am I obliged to answer?" she asked, haughtily, although her voice and lips trembled sadly,
while the bright spot on either cheek burnt
brighter than ever.

" Yes."

" Three months—perhaps more." And she
cleared her throat and vainly tried to steady her
voice.

" You never saw—him—before that time?"

" Never."

" Enough. I now require a promise that you
never willingly—mind, I say willingly—never
willingly see him again."

Cynthia seemed striving to collect her thoughts
ere she answered, slowly, " You yourself have
quite prevented that. There is no need to require
a promise from me."

" I will have no dilly-dallying; no shuffling,"
replied Sir Cyrus, sharply.

" I have never been guilty of so mean an
action," and this time there was but a slight
quavering of the voice.

"Then promise, child. Promise!"

"I am no child. I will not have a promise wrenched from me. I will not!" No she would not. Sir Cyrus saw it, and perplexed how to act, or what to say, he got up and walked the room.

"Cynthia," said he, presently, coming back to where she was, and once more sitting down; "I will not treat you as a child; though mind you are but a child in years, and I might as a father exact obedience, but I will not—I do not. I ask you for your good, your future well being in life, your peace of mind, and mine, to give me this promise."

Yes, her father's peace of mind, her father's pride, but not hers.

"You have never treated me as a daughter," she answered, "you have been totally forgetful of my existence. Had you been as cold as ice to me, I could have borne it better, because the very fact of your being cold would have shown you took, at least, some notice of me; but you have been careless and totally unconcerned, and heedless about me, and yet you wonder, that wanting your love, I—I have valued another's."

Her words struck her father forcibly, like so many deep stabs. He felt the truth of all she said.

"I forgot the lapse of years," he murmured; "forgot all and everything that made life bearable to me--forgot even you. My remorse—my grief at your mother's death—swallowed up all minor things. You do well to remind me of my —not exactly want of love, but want of care of you. I deserve this disobedience on your part; this presumption of those cursed Alywins."

His first words smote her heart, but the latter shut it against him.

"My mother would have loved me had she lived,—cared for me, and never wounded me."

"Your mother, child, never harmed a fly. She loved and cared for all God's creatures. She was gentle and submissive."

"But not submissive if her love for you had been forbidden," said Cynthia.

" She would not have gainsayed me now. My will was her will. She would not have *exacted* this promise from you, but she would have persuaded you, with loving words, such as I have not at command. I loved her passionately—love her still;" and Sir Cyrus' voice trembled and his hand shook, as he shaded his face from Cynthia's gaze. " Give me this promise, child, for your mother's sake, if not for mine."

" Oh, papa!" exclaimed she, her softer and better feelings touched by his words, " oh, papa! forgive me if I have said anything to cause you pain!" and tottering forward, she knelt at his feet, and hid her face on his knees; " and forgive me, too, that I cannot cease to love Frederick Alywin. I love him with all my heart. You cannot, you will not be so cruel, so unkind, as to refuse to sanction it. I will wait; wait any time, so that I may sometimes see him—sometimes hear his voice. I love him, papa! I shall die if you force this promise from me."

The time of trial—the time Frederick Alywin

had spoken of had come. She would speak out, and not be ashamed of her love, but implore her father's mercy, or brave his anger.

"Think of mamma," she went on, "and of how you loved her, and how she might have died had she been denied your love. Oh, papa! if you think of her you must pity me, and not darken my whole life; and I so young—so young," she ended, plaintively.

But Sir Cyrus steeled his heart. He inwardly hated the Alywins as being the cause of his sister's broken health and wasted life. His daughter's determination of loving one of that family, roused his anger, and not his pity. He lifted her from the ground firmly, but gently.

"I cannot grant it, Cynthia,—cannot. Nay, more, I swear I will not. I hate the whole brood of Alywins, one and all!"

She moved away to the door without another word; but Sir Cyrus stood before it, and prevented her opening it.

"I must have that promise," he said.

Cynthia's face flushed, then paled again.

"I will not give it!" she said—"will not!" and her voice faltered strangely. "I am ill, and it is cruel of you to urge me now. Let me go; please let me go."

But Sir Cyrus caught her arm.

"Child! girl!" he cried, exasperated at her refusal; "I *will* have that promise. Do you hear?"

No, she did not hear. Her light form trembled, and then grew heavy in his grasp— heavier still; and when he released her, she slid quietly on to the ground.

Half frightened, Sir Cyrus lifted her in his strong, powerful arms, and carried her away upstairs. As he passed by the large painted window, the light from a lamp hanging there, shone full on Cynthia's face, which looked of an almost death-like hue. Sir Cyrus stopped involuntarily, and placed his hand on her heart, as though to feel its beating, while his own almost stood still the while; then satisfied it was not

death he had to fear, he went on into Cynthia's
room. Nurse was standing half abstractedly at
a table, dipping, every now and then, a cloth into
a basin filled with vinegar and water. She
uttered an exclamation of alarm, as Sir Cyrus
came in and laid his insensible burden on the
bed.

" Miss Cynthia has fainted," said he, as he
went back and closed the door, and then again
drew near his daughter's side.

Nurse hurried over, wringing her hands.

·" Oh, my poor lamb!—my sweet, innocent
lamb!" she cried. " Who has done this?—who
has been so cruel? It wasn't for nothing I saw
the winding sheet in my candle last night. I knew
it was a sign of ill luck, if of nothing worse;
but I never expected such bad luck as this. Poor
darling! poor pet! to think, after all my care, it
should come to this!'

"Come to what?" asked Sir Cyrus, angrily.

" To the worst!" said she—" come to death,
maybe. Feel her hands, Sir Cyrus—feel her

head, and then tell me if it mayn't be death, when they burn like a flame of fire?"

She waited a moment, and then said, " Where did she get that blow on her poor forehead?— not fairly, I'll swear."

Nurse was a privileged person—almost sacred in her master's eyes, as having been his wife's only nurse through her sad illness and death. She spoke to him as none other dared do; she braved his anger, and cared nought for his rage. He heard more truths from her than he cared. He had not courage to meet her eyes, as he replied to her words of, " Where did she get that blow ?"

" She fell down."

" Fell down ! And do you suppose if she had, Sir Cyrus, she wouldn't have come and told me all about it, like she used to when she was a baby, and I kissed the place to make it well. Poor lamb, she never did it by accident. Although she wouldn't tell me how it was done, I know 'twasn't fairly, or she wouldn't have kept it in her poor little heart till it's burst well nigh; and I shouldn't wonder if it was to break; and then—then I pity those as done it, for it'll be murder!" and she looked fiercely at Sir Cyrus, as she chafed her young mistress's hands, and bathed her face and forehead.

"Hold your tongue, woman! You know nothing at all about it."

"I know a good deal too much," said she to herself, as Sir Cyrus left the room, to give orders that Mr. Gibbs should be sent for as speedily as possible.

Mr. Gibbs was one of the surgeons at Broadbelt; for, small as the place was, it boasted of four, all apparently well off; but Mr. Gibbs was the only one who did not visit his patients on foot. Mr. Gibbs had a gig, and an animal scarcely deserving the name of horse, so lean, and bony, and long-eared; its head carried viciously erect, with a short, stumpy tail—hardly deserving the name of tail, its few hairs hardly to be seen at all, he hugged it so tight; while, as to legs, he had none. Yet, notwithstanding all these disadvantages, it was a great day for the Gibbs' when the gig first made its appearance at their door. All day Mrs. Gibbs could settle to nothing; or if she did take her work, it was only to throw it down again, and run to the window, as each carriage, or even cart, rattled by. The small street boys went so far as to cheer Mr. Gibbs, which incensed the horse to such a degree, he resented the affront by kicking in the splash board; and I am afraid to say how many times since that same splash board had not been mended, on account of, as Mr. Gibbs expressed it, that same playful trick. " Splash board again, Pa?" would observe a mischievous young Gibbs, when the gig failed to make its appearance at the usual hour, and its owner had ignominously to visit his patients on foot.

To-day, however, the " turn-out " was in first-rate order, and Mr. Gibbs made quite a victorious entry into Stonycleft, driving up to the door in dashing style; his only regret being, that the darkness prevented anyone from seeing or admiring it but himself.

Sir Cyrus sat in his study, in no very enviable frame of mind, considering what he should do under the difficulty that had overtaken him. Yesterday, Cynthia had been but a child,—to-day, he had been startled into the sudden conviction that she was a woman ; and, moreover, one with as firm a will and purpose as any Bedfield ever had. No wonder her governesses found her difficult to manage. No wonder Miss Castle stooped to play the spy. What a fool he had been to allow his daughter so much latitude! But how was he to guess such a thing as this would happen? Perhaps he ought to have married again ; but his heart revolted at the idea of replacing his lost wife, by marrying any of the girls or women he had seen ; besides, having never entertained such a thought. So Sir Cyrus sat smoking and thinking first one thing and then another, but never finding himself nearer solving the difficulty. Cynthia would never give him this promise, and he must somehow act without it; but how to act puzzled him.

Later on in the evening, Sir Cyrus was told of Mr. Gibbs' arrival, and desired he might be shown into his study.

Mr. Gibbs was a fat, puggy little man, very learned and pompous with most of his patients; but all his bombast vanished before the owner of Stonycleft, as he tried *not* to look what he was, completely awed. Awed at the grandeur of the house; the footmen with their rich liveries and powdered heads; and lastly, at Sir Cyrus himself, and the extreme politeness with which he greeted him.

" Good evening, Mr. Gibbs. I regret the necessity of sending for you so late; but Miss Bedfield's sudden indisposition allowed me no choice. Pray be seated, sir."

Mr. Gibbs sat down nervously, then feeling it was expected he should say something, cleared his throat, as though to help him to regain the

confidence he had gradually been losing ever
since he entered the house.

"Ahem! Sir Cyrus, I would observe first, that
no one can regret more than myself the young
lady's unfortunate and sudden illness; but we
must hope, sir—we must hope that with time
and care Miss Bedfield may recover her usual
health; we have youth, Sir Cyrus—youth as well
as beauty to help us."

This speech did not give the satisfaction Mr.
Gibbs had expected, for, as he drew a long breath
of relief and gratification at having spoken so
well and to the purpose, Sir Cyrus moved impatiently in his chair.

"You have seen Miss Bedfield, sir?"

"I have, Sir Cyrus—and—"

"Excuse me, sir, if I ask you to answer me a·
few questions. Do you think my daughter's a
serious illness?"

"Ahem! I would observe, Sir Cyrus, that Miss
Bedfield's illness is as yet in too early a stage for ·

me to give—ahem!—any positive opinion as to how it may, or may not turn out."

" Is there any fever?"

" Yes ; a good deal.   I should say her pulse was—"

" And the head, sir, and temples, are they cool ?"

" Quite the reverse, Sir Cyrus."

" She may be delirious."

" She will."

" And the blow, the—the accidental blow on the forehead, has that anything to do with my daughter's illness ?"

" The blow, Sir Cyrus, is superficial, and of no consequence.   But I should say—excuse me, Sir Cyrus, I *must* say it," said Mr. Gibbs, seeing his hearer was about to interrupt him again,—" the young lady has had some sudden fright or fall that has greatly shaken the nervous system."

" When do you repeat your visit?" asked Sir Cyrus, rising.

"To-morrow morning. Will seven o'clock be too early?"

"The earlier the better. You have left instructions with the lady up-stairs?"

"Lady! I saw no lady, Sir Cyrus; only the nurse—and a better you could not have or find anywhere."

"Can I offer you any refreshment, after your drive?"

"Thank you, Sir Cyrus, my supper is waiting me at home. Good evening."

Away went Mr. Gibbs, chafing at the reception he had met with from Sir Cyrus. I am afraid his hand was not so gentle with the reins and whip as it ought to have been; certainly his exit from the park was anything but a triumphant one, and as unlike his successful entry—but a short half hour before—as it well could be ; while the unlucky splashboard was so damaged, it scarcely afforded a protection to poor little Mr. Gibbs' legs from the succession of playful tricks of the horse. Certainly, "Let Fly," as the boys had mischievously nicknamed him, was either in the highest of spirits, or otherwise he felt aggrieved at his master's ill temper, and determined to resent it.

CHAPTER VII.

CASTLES IN THE AIR.

Two or three days after these events, Mrs. Alywin
drove over in her small pony-chaise to Friarmarsh, timing her visit so as to arrive about the
time she knew her son would be sitting down to
dinner. But she waited in the drawing-room
some little time, and he did not make his appearance.

How familiar were all the objects to her, and
how large the room seemed after her small one at
Broadbelt. She looked round rather sorrowfully,

remembering how dearly grand she had thought
this same room when her husband first brought
her as a bride to his home, and how much she had
been struck with wonder and admiration at the
size of the large bow window opening on to the
smooth, velvet looking lawn; so different from
the small one in the close, hot back parlour of
her father's shop. Then, as years rolled on, how
gradually she had grown accustomed to its
grandeur and dissatisfied with its common place
look; had teased her husband into putting plate
glass windows instead of the old-fashioned small
squares of glass; and a handsome marble mantle-
piece with large mirror above, and, lastly, the
conservatory at the side window, to shut out the
sight of the kitchen garden and stables.

Mrs. Alywin rose and opened the conservatory
door, a scent of sweet flowers pervading the room
as she did so, appealing strongly to her senses,
and recalling old times, scenes, and faces
forcibly, that she burst into tears. After a while
she got up, settled her cap and bonnet at the glass

over the chimney-piece, and went out on to the lawn.

Crossing to where a gardener was busy at work,

"Good morning, old John"—an appellation bestowed on him when his son, young John, came also to work on the farm. "Where is your master?" asked she.

"'Bout the farm with the young un, ma'am," was the reply.

So Mrs. Alywin strolled away, half-inclined to search for him, but, thinking of her flushed face and recent tears, determined on remaining where she was, and seated herself—prepared to wait patiently—on the garden seat under the ash.

Mrs. Alywin was ill at ease, and evidently worried about something. Her recent tears were not solely caused by the sad remembrance of by-gone times, but were more the result of long pent up emotions hardly restrained, and requiring but a light touch to call them forth. She turned her face to the wind, so as to allow the light summer

air to blow on her face, and remove, if possible,
the traces of the emotion she had given way to;
but there was little time allowed her for recovery,
as almost immediately her son came whistling up
the garden walk. He was a fine, well-grown
young man, taller than the average height of
men, and, although a farmer at heart and soul,
had a certain aristocratic—if I may so express
it—bearing about him. He was much liked and
respected by all those with whom he came in
contact or claimed friendship with; and almost
worshipped on the farm as being, though strict,
yet a kind and generous master. Mrs. Alywin
had reason to be proud of him, but that we know
she was not; her thoughts, feelings, her whole
being in fact, entirely taken up with her gentle-
manly son Fred.

"I heard you were here, mother," said Mr.
Alywin, as he welcomed her.

"I have been waiting some time," she
answered; "I came expecting to find you at
dinner."

"I have dined," he replied. "Having an engagement at three requiring all my wits, I dined early, so as to go to it with a clear head, and wide-awake brain."

"I hope it's nothing vexatious. You don't look well; you seem bothered."

. "That is just it, mother; I am bothered. To tell you the truth—and it's a very mortifying one—I was induced to take shares in a concern that was to double my venture, and, as far as I could see, no risk. But to make the long story short, the thing is a smash, and not only do I lose the shares, but have to pay up besides, and I do not see where the folly will end."

"Well, it will teach you wisdom another time, Percy."

"Yes; but it is a serious loss, mother. I shall have to economise sharp."

Mrs. Alywin winced; she felt she could not have come at a more inopportune moment for the request or favour she had to beg.

"Your father left you well off, Percy. The loss can only inconvenience you a little."

"A little!" he echoed, as he thought of the hundreds of pounds swallowed up. "A little! Well, the best 1 can say is that it will not affect either you or Fred. His money is safely invested in land, which land is improving every year. No, it will not affect Fred."

"Ah! poor Fred," said Mrs. Alywin, in a tone of commiseration.

"Why that sorrowful tone, mother? Is there anything the matter with him?"

"Why, don't you know?" began his mother; "I thought, of course, you knew of his sad accident."

"Accident! What accident? I am quite in the dark."

"Well, I did wonder why you hadn't been to see him. But a few days ago he started for a walk with Charlotte, and it seems they had a quarrel and went off different ways after a bit. Sadly put out he wandered a good long way till he came to the Quarry pits, and there he tried to get some birds' eggs for Charlotte, which, you

know, she is collecting; but somehow, in climb-
a tree, he lost his balance, and fell down one of
the pits, bruising himself dreadfully; his face is
quite altered, you'd hardly know him; so swollen
and such a deep cut across it. He's terribly
shaken, poor fellow, and has been in bed ever
since."

"I never heard a word about it. I'll look in
this evening on my way home."

"But—but I hav'nt told you the worst," continued Mrs. Alywin, trying to stifle her rising
emotion, and quiet her fears as to how he would
take the next piece of information she had to
give; "he—he—well he refuses to become a
clergyman; he says he isn't fit for it; and this,
too, when he was getting on so well, and after
the sight of money it's cost."

"You are right mother, it has cost a good
deal. But, perhaps, Fred may be right. I
thought it a foolish plan from the first. But it
strikes me he has changed his views very suddenly; why I only met him—let me see—last

Wednesday, I think, and then he was looking forward to [going up for his 'little go," and certainly told me he was devoted to his books."

" And so he has been until now."

" Well, mother, you do astonish me!"

" I thought I should," said she, quietly.

" And what does he intend doing ?" asked Mr. Alywin, after a pause.

" I'm half afraid to tell you," replied she.

" Nonsense, mother! I've no jealousy whatever, and if it's to come back here and turn farmer, why I say Amen with all my heart. It's what he ought to have done from the very first— my father wished it.".

" Fred doesn't wish it. You know well enough he never liked a farmer's life."

" Then what, in God's name, mother, does he want now ?"

" He—he—" replied Mrs. Alywin, grandly, but falteringly, " he wants to be an officer."

Mr. Alywin laughed outright; as much as at the—to him—absurd proposal as at his mother's

ludicrous way of putting it. Then, half angry
with himself, he hastened to tender some kind of
apology, by saying,

" Excuse me mother, but surely Fred's head
must be a little muddled from the effects of his
fall. What does Mr. Parker say about it?"

" He hasn't seen him," answered she, crossly ;
" he won't see a doctor ; and Fred's as right in
the head as either you or I ; and," continued Mrs.
Alywin, rather proudly, " I don't see myself that
his wanting to be an officer is anything so very
preposterous. My brother is one of the Volun-
teers, and that's next door to it."

" That's a very different thing," replied Mr.
Alywin, " I am thinking of becoming a Volunteer
myself; but to enter the army! Why, mother,
it is preposterous, say what you will."

" And I don't see it. Why, only look at those
Turners at Cumber; they're nothing but linen-
drapers, yet the son is in the dragoons. I am
sure we are fifty times better up in the world than
they are."

"Yes, mother! but it is not electioneering time. No one is ready to give a bribe for a vote. The idea of a man entering the army under such circumstances is a dishonour, and one that I should blush to be guilty of. Fred has had his start in life, and I should be acting wrongly, now he has begun to put his hand to the plough, to encourage his versatile disposition, or help him in turning back. Depend upon it, he will forget all about this absurd idea in a few days."

"I am sure he won't," replied Mrs. Alywin; "it has been in his head for a long time. He does not think himself good enough, nor wise enough; and although he has got such a lot of pleasant talk, and can write such beautiful letters, he says he is sure he never could write a sermon, or preach it either; and I am sure I should be on pins and needles if he were to break down; and Mrs. Knollys such a constant attendant at church, too; she would be sure to hear him, and 'twit' me about it afterwards; for although she does not think me good enough to visit, she never fails to stop and tell me disagreeables in the street."

" Well, mother, I am sorry for you; but I have very little patience with Fred. I conceive him to be acting badly. Let him give up the church, by all means, if—if distasteful to him ; but this idea of soldiering is little short of madness."

" For my part, I don't see it at all. I only wonder we did not think of his soldiering propensities before. He always has had a hankering that way. Don't you remember how fond he was as a child of his tin soldiers ?"

" I cannot say I do," said Mr. Alywin, smiling in spite of himself; and then added, after a moment's thought, "what do you propose doing about Fred ?"

" Getting him a commission, of course ; and I think, Percival, you might do that for me," said Mrs. Alywin, in an injured tone.

" I, mother ! why I have not a particle of interest. I don't know a single army man. The idea is folly!"

" Not so foolish as you think. How about,— or how would it do to ask Sir Cyrus ?"

" Are you mad, mother ?" said Mr. Alywin, while an angry flush spread over his face ; " or have you forgotten his father's insult to my father—your husband ?"

"No," said Mrs. Alywin, doggedly ; " I have not forgotten anything of the kind."

" And yet, in the face of it, you wish me to stoop to ask a favour," said Mr. Alywin, bitterly ; " and get kicked out for my pains as—as—others have been. Are you in your sane senses, mother ?"

" Yes ; I was never more so ; but you make such a rumpus about a trifle, I hardly know what I am doing, or what I want to say. I know Sir Cyrus insulted your father, and that is the very reason why you ask a right, not a favour of him, for I am sure he owes us some reparation. Besides, you need not ask it at all, you can write to

him, and I won't mind betting ten chances to
one but what he will be ashamed to say no."

"Did Fred advise you to this?" asked Mr.
Alywin.

"No."

"Then I am sorry that in thought I half sus-.
pected him of being the instigator. And now,
mother," said Mr. Alywin, rising, "let us dismiss this subject for ever! The Bedfields may
be proud, but by heaven! they shall never find
an Alywin base enough to ask a favour of them."

Disheartened, but in no wise discouraged,
although perhaps a little ashamed of herself,
Mrs. Alywin returned home, plotting as she
went how she could manage to get her son's commission, and was obliged at last to confess unwillingly, as she alighted at her own door, that
the task she had set herself to accomplish was at
the best almost hopeless.

"There's a note come for you, ma'am," said the
servant girl.

"A note! Where from?"

"The young man wouldn't say, ma'am; but I think 'twas one of the stable boys up to Stonycleft brought it."

Mrs. Alywin stared at the servant girl as though she were demented; and went into the little parlour, scarcely knowing whether she walked on her head or her heels.

There lay the note on the table close by her work; a small common-place note it looked, the address written in anything but an aristocratic style, the letters so clumsily formed and the strokes so thick. Mrs. Alywin was disappointed; and still more so, when she saw a small bunch of flowers, neatly gummed down, stood in the place of the Bedfield crest on the back of the envelope.

" From Stonycleft," said she, as she broke the seal; " absurd!" and crestfallen and disappointed she proceeded to read it.

It was short and its contents mystifying.

"Stonycleft,

"July 10th.

"MADAM,

"I have something of the greatest importance to propose to you. It is also essential that I should not be seen at your house. If not asking too much would you oblige me with a private interview *here* some day this week, at your earliest convenience? Might I also beg the favour of a reply by post. Trusting you will pardon my addressing you, on account of the urgency of the case,

"I am,

"Madam,

"Yours faithfully,

"CYRUS BEDFIELD."

A mist swam before Mrs. Alywin's eyes. She felt as if she were going to faint.

"Good gracious," she said; "what can the

man want? I hope it's nothing improper, so secret and tight as he wants to keep things; really it makes me feel quite queerish. Perhaps he's taken a fancy to me. Poor Mr. Alywin used to say I was a very good-looking woman for my age, and then how Sir Cyrus stared last Sunday in church; I said it was at me, although Charlotte declared it was at the new painted window behind us. I wonder what she'll say when I tell her? But there that's the worst of it, I must not tell her, but keep it all to myself."

She took up pen and ink and prepared to write an answer, a work of some time and no little trouble to her, but it was—after a good many corrections and wasted sheets of paper—written, and ran thus—

" Broadbelt,
" July 10th.

" SIR CYRUS BEDFIELD,

"I shall be happy to call on you to-morrow at three o'clock, and have no doubt we

shall be able to arrange matters satisfactorily,
although in my lonely position as a widow, I
feel rather nervous at coming to your house
alone.

"I am,

"Sir Cyrus,

"Yours truly,

"SARAH ALYWIN."

"There," said she, as she folded it up, "I
think that will do nicely. There's nothing to
take offence at, and lots of encouragement if—if
he really intends to offer," and putting it into her
pocket she walked to the post office at the other
end of the town as though she were treading on
air, settling much to her own satisfaction that, a
Lady Bedfield was decidedly above and superior
to a general's wife, a plain Mrs. Knollys, and
building castles in the air at every step she
took.

CHAPTER VIII.

FACE TO FACE.

For three days Cynthia lay in a kind of stupor, taking no notice of external objects, but on the fourth, when Sir Cyrus returned from church, she was—as little Mr. Gibbs prognosticated she would be—delirious. No need then to tell nurse what had caused such illness when she heard from her young mistress's lips, over and over again, the terrible scene down by the river. Nurse not only looked daggers at her master when he came into the room, but her tongue every now and then spoke volumes, although but in short, concise words; yet they were turned towards him, or had a point in them, hitting like so many sharp arrows.

Sir Cyrus' heart smote him as he listened to his daughter's ravings. Not for the passion he had given way to before her—that he did not regret; but for the careless, negligent way in which he had looked after her. Had he but been more mindful, more strict, all this anxiety would have been spared both him and her; and again how bitterly he cursed the Alywins for having a second time brought shame on his house.

Sir Cyrus did not believe his daughter to be deeply attached to Frederick Alywin; he argued that she was but sixteen, and at that age the heart was like wax; she would forget him as easily as she had taken a fancy to him, for in so short a time her feelings for him could be neither very strong, deep, nor lasting : still he was uneasy, and more than ever determined that some decisive steps should be taken towards putting an end to the dangerous intimacy.

" Has Miss Castle seen Miss Cynthia to-day?" asked Sir Cyrus, of nurse.

" No, Sir Cyrus ; nor yet for many days. Mr. Gibbs' orders were, the fewer the better; but I expect she'll be coming here now before long, when she finds out it isn't the measles."

" Measles ! " echoed Sir Cyrus, in astonishment.

" Yes, I took it upon myself to tell her 'twas the measles, so as to keep the room free of her. In such a case as this, I thought it best to be rid of her and her prying eyes. No one knows of the *blow* but the doctor and us three."

Sir Cyrus winced as he looked at the dark blue mark standing out so prominently on the clear, white forehead ; and, almost with a woman's tenderness, he raised his daughter's head, as nurse gathered up the soft fair hair and smoothed it over the pillow out of the way, but only to be again in the same entangled state shortly after, as Cynthia tossed about so restlessly to and fro.

"You will take Miss Castle in hand, sir, and prevent her coming here," said nurse, as Fred's name fell in endearing terms from the sick girl's lips.

"She *must* be prevented," replied her master.

"So I'm thinking, Sir Cyrus. Best not let every body in the house know the outs and ins of the case."

"Has she mentioned any name? Miss Cynthia, I mean."

"Only the one you have just heard, sir; and I'm sure it makes my poor heart bleed to hear her call on the gentleman to save her. She's been in sore trouble and fright, Sir Cyrus, and shudders all over when she calls your name. If —if she dies what'll her poor nurse do?" and the tears started in her eyes, and fell one by one on the bed.

Sir Cyrus breathed more freely. As yet all was safe. Nurse had no clue to anything; besides,

if she did hit upon one, she was too attached
to his house to make a talk of it.   But Miss
Castle was different.   She was a shrewd woman,
and were she to hear the wild talk nurse did,
would be sure to ferret out to whom the name
belonged, and the bare idea of *that*, filled Sir
Cyrus' heart with rage.   A Bedfield at death's
door for the sake of a low bred farmer's son, and
an Alywin into the bargain !   It was not to be
borne or tolerated, and should be prevented, and
put a stop to.

Shortly afterwards Miss Castle was summoned
to Sir Cyrus' study.

She came in looking her best.   Her rich dark
hair drawn off her face, to give that height to her
forehead which it had not.   Her large grey eyes
bent downwards, so as to show off the dark, somewhat short lashes.   A light coloured muslin, very
full and long, floating about her tall figure.   She
looked two-and-thirty, but might have been
more, though if she was, her age was well con-
cealed.

Shě carried her small head proudly, although she stood meekly before Sir Cyrus, until he rose and offered her a chair.

"I have thought it right to return you this book by my own hand, in case of accidents;" said Sir Cyrus, taking a book from off the table beside him, and handing it Miss Castle.

"Thank you, Sir Cyrus."

"At the same time," he continued, "I beg to suggest that I think it would be better and more correct did I return it to the librarian."

"I am sure you are right, Sir Cyrus, and I know I am very wrong in wishing it; but I would rather give it back myself;" not for the world would Miss Castle let Sir Cyrus and the librarian come in contact.

"As you please, madam," he replied; "I merely suggested what I thought the correct thing."

"It is a French book, and French books are so difficult to choose; one never exactly can tell their tone until one reads them. You saw it was French, Sir Cyrus?" said she, trying to find out whether he understood the language, or had been able to master any of its contents.

He set her mind at rest at once.

" Certainly, and I can only trust from the character of the story that my daughter has not read any part of it.   Its tendency is bad, and the whole tenor of the book immoral." Sir Cyrus spoke angrily, and without consideration. " Any future books, madam, must be selected by myself, or at least pass through my hands. I am surprised Mr. Fanshaw should have dared send such a book. I see he has not had the face to paste a printed form on the back."

Miss Castle trembled. Would or did Sir Cyrus question her veracity? He left her in doubt; almost immediately changing the subject to his daughter.

" Have you seen Miss Bedfield to-day?"

" Oh! Sir Cyrus," replied she, clasping her hands, " I am so sorry, so very sorry. I would have nursed her willingly, only too willingly; but

I have never had the measles. Had it been any other disorder, I would have been at her bedside day and night."

"Miss Bedfield is not suffering from measles. The symptons are more those of typhus," said Sir Cyrus, drily; while he raised his eyes to hers to judge how she would receive the startling announcement.

Startling it was to her—most startling. So much so, that for once she forgot to act a part, and spoke naturally.

"Good gracious! sir. How very dreadful!"

She was afraid of it, then! So much the better.

"You will see that there is now a reason—a more weighty reason—why you should absent yourself from the sick room; indeed, it would be advisable you should not approach that wing at all; or perhaps, you would prefer leaving Stony-cleft for a time?"

Leave Stonycleft? Leave her hopes, her wishes? Allow another to supplant her there, and perhaps carry off the prize? No. Better brave death than that. She at once put on her most beseeching look.

" Oh ! don't send me away; please do not send me away, Sir Cyrus !" pleaded she, earnestly. " I will take every precaution. I will run no risk. But indeed, I have no home to go to now —or at least just yet, so suddenly."

" No home? You have the one from which you came, surely?"

" The lady with whom I lived is dead," and Miss Castle looked touchingly mournful; "and I am as you know, Sir Cyrus, an orphan. I am now a lone woman, with not a soul to care for or take care of me."

" Very sad," replied Sir Cyrus; " and my dear madam, in that case, I think you had better risk infection and remain at Stonycleft."

" Oh! thank you ! You are so very good—so kind ! " said Miss Castle, in an impassioned tone.

" But recollect, on the one condition, that you

do not go near my daughter's room. It will not do to have two invalids to nurse."

" I promise—promise faithfully," and, indeed, at that moment, with the fear of typhus, there was little danger of her breaking her promise.

"Then it is settled you remain," said Sir Cyrus, " on the one condition that you keep away from my daughter's room ; any infringement of this promise, and I am to conclude that you wish to give up your engagement here ?"

" Yes, Sir Cyrus. But I shall be very dull. Oh ! so dull. How I shall miss my pupil, and especially of an evening ; then, indeed, I shall be quite alone, but the summer evenings are short;" and Miss Castle sighed, and looked handsomer than ever.

Sir Cyrus could not resist that pleading look.

" Perhaps, Miss Castle, you would prefer coming down to the drawing-room of an evening. Pray do so if you feel inclined, and you think it would be less dull. I shall be glad of some one to make tea for me now Cynthia is ill."

Miss Castle could not prevent a slight flushing of the face, although she pressed her finger nails almost into the flesh, as her hands clasped each other in her lap. The joyous light that danced for a second in her eyes she hid by looking fixedly on the ground. When she raised them again there was a sorrowful look on her face.

" How very, very kind you are. So isolated, so wretchedly lonely as I sometimes feel, and so unused in my life to a pitying word, your—your words quite overpower me," and Miss Castle pressed her handkerchief to her eyes as though to hide her grief.

" There, there, my dear lady," said Sir Cyrus, disarmed at the sight of her tears, " pray do not. I am sure I had no idea you were unhappy. It grieves me much."

" Thank you—thank you for so many kind words. But—but you will excuse me, I am sure ;" and with a half-smothered sob Miss Castle rose and went away swiftly, but gracefully.

"A fine woman," said Cyrus, as the door
closed, "a monstrous fine woman. A woman
that could act the part of Norma to perfection.
A first-rate woman for the stage. She would not
stoop to the subterfuge of spraining *her* ancle;
she's above such petty meanness. She would
lay her plans deeper and surer. I must be
watchful and on my guard, and see as little of
her as I can or she might catch me in her net before I knew where I was. Hang the woman's
tears! but for those I should have been as cold
as stone, notwithstanding her pleading looks.
She will not go into the sick room; I effectually
prevented that; or if she does, and hears anything, I have always the book to hold over her.
What a fool I was to let her have it again!
That was a wrong move; but any trespassing or
peaching on her part, and she goes without a
character; tears or no tears, I swear it."

And then Sir Cyrus' thoughts wandered towards the Alywins; all of whom save Frederick
Alywin he had seen that day in church.

"The mother's a fool," said he, aloud, "and the only one I can venture to tackle, if she can only keep a quiet tongue in her head." And after a little more consideration he took pen and paper, and wrote the note which we have already read, and which caused poor Mrs. Alywin so many heart flutterings and agitation.

CHAPTER IX.

A LADY TO SEE YOU, SIR CYRUS.

ALTHOUGH the Alywins' seat in church was in
view of the Bedfield pew, Sir Cyrus had never
taken the trouble to notice anyone of the party;
for what had he, with his aristocratic notions and
high blood, to do with a set of parvenues, who had
once boldly dared the thought of allying themselves to his house? But now he had a motive
in marking them with his searching glance, and
Mrs. Alywin was right in her supposition that
Sir Cyrus had stared at her and not at the

painted window during the last Sunday's service. Sir Cyrus *had* looked at her—looked at all and each in turn, striving to find the one likely to prove the most amenable to his wishes, or be used as a tool.

Mr. Alywin, with his fearless, truthful bearing, was out of the question. Charlotte would do better, but something in her soft, clear eye, as it once, during the service, met his, deterred him, and he decided on Mrs. Alywin. She looked vulgar and commonplace, and, if properly managed, inoffensive, and with a little tact and well-timed flattery—than which none knew better than Sir Cyrus how to offer—it might be done. Hence the note to Mrs. Alywin—for he felt sure Fred would not mention his thrashing— which had brought a reply favourable to his wishes, and he now awaited her visit somewhat impatiently. Impatiently because she was behind time, and Sir Cyrus hated unpunctuality, besides, having laid his plans he was anxious to commence the siege, and lay the mine

which, when lighted—if it did light—should ex-
plode in his favour; so he restlessly walked the
room, or stood at the window and gazed down
the drive more irritably still, or pulled out his
watch, which was even some few minutes faster
than the great clock of Stonycleft, and eased his
mind a little by allowing his ill temper to ex-
pend itself in heaping abuse on her. "Why
could not a woman be punctual? The failing
must be born in her; for, as far as his experience
went, no woman ever was punctual." Then he
modified this latter assertion by suddenly remembering that Miss Castle always came to time,
and was about the only woman he knew who did,
a trait in his governess's character which raised
her somewhat suddenly in his estimation, and
set his thoughts wandering towards her rather
favourably, in the midst of which the door
opened, and with the words "A lady to see you,
Sir Cyrus," Mrs. Alywin rustled in.

She was dressed in her black moiré, and large
gold chain, which latter glistened in the light

from the opposite window, and trembled—almost
shook—above the wearer's heavy respiration, for
what with her early dinner and warm walk Mrs.
Alywin was very much out of breath, while her
rosy, good-tempered face looked rosier than ever.
She did not appear in the least awed, as poor
little Mr. Gibbs had done, neither did she seem
nervous. She had made up her mind as she came
along to get her son's commission by hook or by
crook, whether Sir Cyrus "popped" or no, and
ask it—if needs be—in right of the injury and
insult her husband had once received, so that
both Sir Cyrus and herself, without the other
being aware of it, were aiming at the same point,
namely, Frederick Alywin's removal from Broadbelt.

"I am expecting the honour of a visit from
Mrs. Alywin," began Sir Cyrus.

"Yes, Sir Cyrus, that's me. I hope I have
not kept you waiting; but I could not get away
sooner on account of dinner being late; servants
are so unpunctual, and then it's such a tremen-

dous long journey from the town for those who
are not accustomed to it. I might have come in
Percival's chaise, but as you said the visit was
to be private I walked it, and very hot I found
it, Sir Cyrus, as I dare say you see?"

"Not so, my dear madam," replied Sir Cyrus,
feeling a compliment was expected. "Indeed, if
I might be permitted, I should say that the walk,
tiring as you may have found it, has decidedly
not proved unbecoming; I never saw you looking
better."

"Oh! Sir Cyrus, how can you! Why you
have never seen me until now. This is our first
introduction."

"Pardon me, madam, I have seen you often.
You are one not easily overlooked, or when once
seen forgotten. Allow me," and he attempted to
take her hand and lead her to a chair.

"Fie! Sir Cyrus; you are too bold;" and she
playfully slapped his hand.

"Nay, madam, I would be bolder if I dared.
Will you not be seated?"

"I don't know whether I ought to sit down.
·1 made up my mind as I came along that I would
only stay five minutes, but you are so pressing,
Sir Cyrus—so very pressing—that I don't see
how I can well refuse," and Mrs. Alywin seated
herself rather close to Sir Cyrus, and spread out
her black moiré ostentatiously. "A widow's is
such a delicate position—one everybody's mouth
wags at. So exposed to insult and suspicion,"
said she, hesitatingly.

"Such a lonely position commands my highest
respect, especially when it has been, as in your
case, it must have been one of choice."

"Quite right, Sir Cyrus. I might have married again before my poor husband was well cold
in his grave;" and a vision of the fat butcher,
her early love, who lived next door to her father's
shop, crossed her mind. Well for her she had
not listened to his tempting offer; and oh! how
jealous would he be, could he but see her
closeted, and on such intimate terms, with the
proud Sir Cyrus Bedfield.

"I can easily believe it, madam," returned Sir Cyrus, in reply, "and I have no doubt many times since then. You deserve the highest praise for such exemplary conduct, such devotion to the one loved memory is rarely met with," and he stroked his long moustaches, perhaps to hide a smile.

"Not but what I might be tempted. We are all of us, at the best, but frail creatures. I might love another just as well as I did poor Mr. Alywin," and she gave Sir Cyrus a sly glance, meant to be encouraging.

Sir Cyrus was getting a little perplexed, for although Mrs. Alywin tried to appear shy and nervous, she fixed her small black eyes on him in a most unpleasant way, and he began to wish himself well out of the business, which, to say the least was growing uncomfortable. What if she were a designing woman after all his caution, and he have to defend himself as best he could against her attacks !

"Suppose we commence the little business you

want to talk to me about at once, Sir Cyrus ; it is awkward being closeted up here so long."

" No possible scandal, madam, can arise from your visiting me at my house. I regret having put you to the trouble and inconvenience of coming; but as to character you are as safe as—as—"

" A nun," suggested Mrs. Alywin.

" My daughter, I would have said. She would I am sure, have welcomed you here with pleasure ; but I regret to say she is ill—very ill."

This was said in Sir Cyrus' stiffest manner, while a shade crossed his face as he mentioned Cynthia.

" Dear me! I *am* sorry. But she always struck me as looking delicate. I dare say we can manage very well without her ; children are so apt to be in the way. Is Miss Bedfield very ill?"

" I am very anxious about her."

" Boys as well as girls are a sore trouble at times, as well as a great blessing. I am in a sea of trouble about my son Fred."

"Indeed!" said Sir Cyrus, with a slight start. "If I can help you in any way pray command my services."

"You can help me a good deal if you like. But suppose you commence business first. I mean your reason for sending for me, to-day, Sir Cyrus."

"It concerns the son you mention. I am anxious, through him, to heal up old wounds."

"Poor fellow, he is wounded enough, I am sure; all covered as he is with scratches and bruises, through falling down a quarry pit out bird's egg hunting, for a girl he is very fond of."

"What girl, madam?" and Sir Cyrus' face flushed angrily.

"My niece, Charlotte. I call her my niece, but she isn't. She is on'y a connection, and a distant one, too. She will have money by-and-bye, and I hope Fred will marry her. But he says he has other views, more's the pity!"

"More's the pity, indeed, madam!" and Sir

Cyrus compressed his lips and walked the room angrily, as was his wont when excited.

Why the man was a scoundrel as well as ambitious. Was it possible he had been trifling with his daughter's feelings? To have loved her was bad enough, but to have dared deceive her! The thought galled his pride to its core, while a feeling of contempt filled his heart for his daughter, who was even now it might be, dying for the sake of a worthless, low bred, beardless boy. But was it possible this Alywin had deceived her? Was not the idea preposterous and unlikely? Sir Cyrus calmed himself and sat down again.

"Is your son very fond of this girl you mention?"

"No, Sir Cyrus; between you and I, I don't think he cares a brass—" she would have said button, but recollecting her son's reproof, corrected herself, "a brass farthing for her."

Sir Cyrus' brow cleared.

"I would provide for that son, madam."

"Provide for him, Sir Cyrus!" and Mrs. Alywin's astonishment was visibly expressed on his face; "you *do* surprise me!" and she drew a deep breath of gratification at the apparently easy accomplishment of her wishes.

" I did not think it would have been deemed a matter of surprise. I, madam, whatever your family may have done, have felt the animosity, the bitter feeling existing between us with—with —regret. The mistake, the wrong may have proceeded from us, but the provocation was great. 1 will not enter into particulars, or rake up old feelings; but simply state that my daughter's serious illness has led me to think more deeply still on these matters, and always with sorrow and—and—"

" Remorse?" suggested Mrs. Alywin.

" I would make atonement, madam," said Sir Cyrus, haughtily. " Heal old feuds if possible, by providing for your son, the young man you mention. He is, I believe, anxious to enter the church. I will get him a chaplaincy abroad."

"I would not part with him for the world!" said Mrs. Alywin, vehemently. "Why I might have him torn in pieces by wild beasts, or scalped by savages!"

"Pshaw!" said Sir Cyrus, impatiently.

"You may 'pshaw!' where you will, Sir Cyrus, but I have heard of worse things than that happening. Why he might marry a black woman, and bring home a lot of pickaninies, as they call them. Good gracious! only think; and I who am so frightened of negroes that I can't bear even to see the screnaders. I was threatened as a child of having a black man sent after me if I was naughty; and I have never been able to bear the sight of one of them since; even talking of them makes me feel quite faint."

And Mrs. Alywin leant back in her chair, and tried to seem ill; look it she could not, her face being far too heated.

"If this is what you call providing for Fred, Sir Cyrus," continued she, fanning herself violently with her pocket-handkerchief, "he'll do very well without your providing; besides he is not going into the church at all; he has set his face against it entirely; and it is this determination of his that has so upset me; after, as I told my eldest son, the sight of money his going to college has cost."

" What does he intend doing, madam? I suppose he will not remain idle?"

" Idle! no. He is going into the army; and if you really want to give him a helping hand, Sir Cyrus, why you could not do better than get him a commission," said Mrs. Alywin, point-blank.

The army! why it was more easily managed than the chaplaincy. What so easy as to get him into a regiment either abroad, or on the eve of going there? Still Sir Cyrus would not appear to acquiesce too readily.

" I will consider the proposition, madam. There are difficulties, of course, in the way; not but what I think I might overcome them; at all events I will try. There is one great difficulty that

strikes me, even at starting ; namely, your son.
Will he accept the commission at my hands ?"

" Of course he will, and only be too glad.
He has no foolish scruples like Percival. You
get it, Sir Cyrus, and I will answer for it he
will take it. Besides I need not tell him who
gives it him. I shall keep the matter as close
as possible, you may be sure, for between you and
I, if my elder son knew of it, he would be as
likely as not, to throw the commission in your
face. He's very vindictive against you all."

Sir Cyrus rose haughtily and impatiently.

" I will no longer trespass on your time,
madam. I will write about the commission at
once, and let you know the result as soon as it
reaches me."

" Thank you, Sir Cyrus. I am sure it is very
good of you ; and if—I don't say there is—but if
there is anything I can do for you in return, I am
sure, or at least, I think you need not be afraid
to ask it of me," said Mrs. Alywin, meaningly,

and, as she thought, in her most insinuating tone.

"Some day, my dear madam, I may claim your promise, may possibly ask a favour at your hands. But now my daughter's unfortunate state of health forbids it."

"Ah! true, Sir Cyrus," said Mrs. Alywin, rising and putting on her glove, which she had purposely taken off in the hopes that he might have been tempted to squeeze her hand. "Poor young lady! we must not forget her."

And having no further excuse for delaying her departure Mrs. Alywin took Sir Cyrus' proffered arm, and he led her out along the stately, but to Mrs. Alywin's eyes, dismal loooking galleries, which she felt convinced contained a ghost in every corner, and certainly behind the heavy crimson drapery of the painted window. Sir Cyrus walked with heavy tread and so long a stride that poor little Mrs. Alywin had every now and then to take little short runs to keep

up with him, while the unwonted exertion made
her so out of breath, that she could not have
put a sentence together had she tried.   Perhaps Sir Cyrus did it purposely to avoid further
conversation.

When they reached the hall door Sir Cyrus
bade her adieu quite affably, and with no little
empressement of manner, and certainly *did* press
her hand at parting; but his object was to con-
ciliate and win her over to his side as much as
possible.

His warmth of manner excited Mrs. Alywin to
an unusual degree, nor had she proceeded far before she tore off her glove and kissed the mark
left on her finger by the impression of his
ring.

"What a stately, noble looking man he is!"
exclaimed she; "and certainly smitten, only his
daughter's illness—a most unfortunate illness for
me—prevented him, as he said, from speaking
out.   I am not a bit afraid of him, not a bit; not
half as much as I am of those dark passages.   If

I do become my lady—and why shouldn't I?—I'll
have some windows knocked here and there, and
put in plate glass instead of those little panes,
just like those I made Mr. Alywin have at Friarmarsh. I can't bear dark places, they always
give me the horrors. And I'll have a black and
white lap-dog, and make one of those men with
floured heads carry it about for me. And I'll
have a violet velvet dress made with a train, ever
so long behind, for it couldn't catch the dirt if I
drove, and call on Mrs. Knollys with a handsome cloak trimmed with jet and lace, a good
quarter of a yard longer than hers ; and instead
of accepting her two fingers, I'd keep my hands
in my muff, if it was winter, and make her my
very grandest courtesy, and toss up my head fifty
times higher than she does !" and Mrs. Alywin
commenced a series of courtesies and gesticulations
quite ludicrous to behold, and somewhat startling
and mystifying to Miss Castle, who had dodged
and followed her thus far unseen.

Miss Castle, always on the watch, had viewed

Mrs. Alywin's visit to Stonycleft with doubt and suspicion. What business had she there?—she of all women, on account of the bitter feeling existing between the two families.

Miss Castle made up her mind to fathom the mystery; and with this intention waited about the park until Mrs. Alywin came out; when, seeing she made for the plantation, through which there was a short cut into Broadbelt, Miss Castle took the private path through the plantation, by which she must reach the stile leading into it before Mrs. Alywin could come up, for she was determined at all hazards to get speech of her. This accomplished, she left the rest to chance.

An accident favoured Miss Castle's views, for as Mrs. Alywin with some difficulty clambered over the stile her dress caught in a nail or slip of wood, and she stood unable to extricate it.

" My goodness ! here's a fix !" exclaimed she. " It's just as well I'm out of sight of the house. What a predicament if Sir Cyrus only happened to come by. Well, it can't be helped ; I am not going to tear my moiré. Perhaps somebody will come this way. I shall wait and see at all events," and very philosophically she leant against the stile.

Miss Castle thought it time to draw near.

"Are you going over the stile?" asked she.

"I *am* over, or at least all but my dress, which I shall be obliged if you will get off the nail where it's hitched, and I beg you will not tear it, if you please," said Mrs. Alywin, who, having recognised in Miss Castle the governess of Stony-cleft, of which place she might some day become the mistress, determined on showing off a few airs.

"I will endeavour not to tear it," replied Miss Castle; "but it is very securely caught. There! I think that will do."

"Thank you," said Mrs. Alywin, shaking herself straight, and looking with no little jealousy and distrust at Miss Castle's handsome face.

What if Sir Cyrus admired her, and she were to cut her out? These kind of people were always so sly and manœuvring! She would walk with her and sift her as she would powdered sugar.

"Are you going home?" asked she of Miss Castle.

" No, I am going for a walk."

" Then if it's all the same to you, perhaps you would not mind keeping me company across the fields. It's such a lonely road, and I am terribly afraid of cows."

" I am not very brave; I have always lived a town life until now."

" Many's the scolding I have had from poor Mr. Alywin about my fears, but all of no use. I always was, and always shall be timid. I am speaking to Sir Cyrus' governess, I think?"

" Miss Bedfield's," corrected Miss Castle.

" It's all the same. Sir Cyrus engaged you, and I suppose will dismiss you if you don't suit; so I dare say you try hard to keep in his good graces. Don't you?"

" Sir Cyrus seems perfectly satisfied with me."

" Vain thing !" thought Mrs. Alywin, angrily.

" What a fine, noble-looking man he is !" said Mrs. Alywin, aloud, returning to the charge ; " so affable.　Do you see much of him ?"

" We meet every day."

" How dangerous !" thought Mrs. Alywin, again.

" Is he very friendly ?"

" Sufficiently so to take my part if need be."

" What a nice house it is ! so compact with every comfort ; and so snug.　I was closeted there with him nearly an hour just now."

" I have been alone with him but seldom ; and never longer than five minutes at a time.　People are so apt to talk."

" Is that a hit at me ?" exclaimed Mrs. Alywin, bridling up.

" I did not so intend it."

" It's a story, and you know it ; when I said I

had been alone with him more than an hour! But there, I suppose you are jealous."

" Jealous! How absurd!"

" It is not absurd. You'd give the world to be ' my lady,' and you know it."

" Whether I would or no, I have a far greater chance than you!" said Miss Castle, meaningly, and with loss of temper.

" I deny it," returned Mrs. Alywin, wrathfully; " widows are always considered quite irresistible."

" *Young* widows," replied Miss Castle, satirically.

" *Young!* I'd have you to know I'm not a grandmother yet. *Young!* I'd thank you to recollect my son Fred is only a trifle older than Sir Cyrus' daughter. You may think yourself a *young* woman, but I'll back myself against you any day; and more than that if I'd the run of the house as you have, I'd be ' my lady ' before the year was out."

" I will take your advice and try," replied

Miss Castle, in a tone anything but conciliatory, and which roused Mrs. Alywin's ire still more.

"I'll let Sir Cyrus know your modest intentions," said she.

"And I will take care, ma'am, he never sees you again. He shall not if I can prevent it! I'll tell him now you are angling for him! An old thing like you! Why you ought to be ashamed of yourself!" said Miss Castle, angrily.

"Look at home!" replied Mrs. Alywin, as Miss Castle turned on her heel and walked rapidly away. "Look at home!" called she again in a high-pitched voice; "I thought you were a bold young woman when I met you at the stile; but now, if you wish to know my opinion, it's this: That you are a bad, good-for-nothing hussy! and I shall live;—mark my words—to see you in the dirt!" and she kicked some hard bits of earth with her boot, after Miss Castle, as though to illustrate her words.

Miss Castle stopped, and facing her for a moment, snapped her fingers derisively; then, with a laugh that echoed through Mrs. Alywin's heart, she turned and walked hurriedly to the stile, over which she went as lightly as a feather.

Mrs. Alywin wrathfully turned her back on her new enemy and pursued her way homewards, passing within a yard of a cow peacefully grazing in her path, and which in her perturbed, pre-occupied state of mind, she never saw !

CHAPTER X.

NURSE CONQUERED.

THE evening of Mrs. Alywin's visit, Sir Cyrus, dissatisfied with Mr. Gibbs, sent for a London physician.

The great man came; charged a small fortune for coming; slightly altered the treatment, and gave his opinion that the case—though one of great danger—was not of necessity hopeless. He spoke favourably of Mr. Gibbs' management, who was now allowed to pursue his own course with the patient, unmolested either by nurse's

constant fussing or the baronet's haughty,
mistrustful look.

Mr. Gibbs had hoped confidently from the first,
and when in a few days Cynthia's illness did take
a turn, the little man, much to his astonishment
found his hands cordially and warmly grasped in
those of Sir Cyrus. Surely so great a condescen-
sion was an ample reward for all Mr. Gibbs'
anxieties, and latterly sleepless nights.

.While her pupil was ill, Miss Castle had it all
her own way down stairs, spending her evenings
—as Sir Cyrus had suggested she should—in the
drawing-room.—But as for company, it was
equally as dull for her as the sitting-room up
stairs, as Sir Cyrus gave her none of his, his
daughter's illness being an excuse for taking his
coffee in his study. But latterly, having no
further plea for absenting himself, he submitted,
at first cautiously, and at length almost wholly, to
the dangerous company and ensnaring fascinations
of his attractive governess.

Mrs. Alywin had not been to Stonycleft again.

Her maternal anxieties regarding Fred were at an end; Sir Cyrus, in about a week's time, having sent her a letter promising her her son's commission.

Attributing this sudden coldness on his part to Miss Castle's agency she determined on having a rap at her in her answer back. Thanking him for his kindness, she warned him to beware of a wolf in sheep's clothing, not very far removed from his own family circle. She could not *write* more explicitly, although she would not mind—if Sir Cyrus wished it—calling and explaining herself more fully; but this Sir Cyrus did *not* wish, and so with this little piece of vengeance she was for the present obliged to rest content.

Frederick Alywin had recovered his thrashing, but he rose from his bed an altered being. He had been but a boy on the morning that Sir Cyrus had come across him; now, his whole nature was changed. He was a man, with hot revengeful feelings burning within him; such feelings as a week ago he knew not he possessed. The wounds

inflicted by Sir Cyrus were not alone outward,
they burnt and raged inwardly, tearing his very
heart-strings. Revenge he had read of—heard
of, but until now never felt how sweet it must
be! He would never rest until it was his; until
he had made Sir Cyrus' heart as sore as his own.
His love for Cynthia seemed as nought to the
fiery feelings that scorched him, and only that a
softer mood came over him when her image crossed
his mind, he would have believed he had ceased
to love her altogether.

· Breaking the matter of the commission to Fred
in his present state, Mrs. Alywin found no easy
task, and far more difficult than she had led Sir
Cyrus to suppose; his first question being as to
who gave it? His next that Sir Cyrus had been
the donor. Mrs. Alywin prevaricated, remon-
strated, but all to no purpose; he disbelieved
her utterly.

" Don't tell any more stories about it, mother,
as whether he gave it or no, I'll take it! and for
this reason—that I can injure him more deeply

by taking it, than by refusing it; and injure him,
so help me God! I will!'"

It troubled Mrs. Alywin to think that both her
sons were so revengefully inclined, and she began to think herself a most miserable woman, and
they the most ungrateful and undutiful of sons.
After this threat of Fred's she sat down quietly,
and had a good cry, going about her household
duties afterwards with swelled eyes, and so doleful
a face, that all in the house felt miserable in the
absence of her cheery look and pleasant chat.
All except Fred, who walked about with his
hands in his pockets whistling lively airs, thinking little of her who was even now, as it might
be said, only just removed from death's door for
his sake.

Cynthia progressed but slowly, and could only,
at the expiration of a week, be moved on to the
sofa in her own room; that exertion bringing
with it so deadly a faintness that nurse thought
her young mistress's last hour was come.

Nurse had as yet not lost all anxiety, although

her nights were no longer passed in doleful sighs
or her days in tears and fidgets. The latter were
out of the question, seeing Cynthia could hardly
bear the rustle of her dress; so she was forced
to sit quiet, however restless her mind might be;
and nurse fidgetted greatly in her mind; it was
in a constant state of unquiet and anxiety. She
had gleaned enough during that terrible illness to
make her heart sore. The fact of her young
mistress' love,—unsuspected until now,—the ever
constant cry from the sick girl's lips during those
dreadful days and nights of delirium, of
" Frederick!—Frederick Alywin!"—one of a
race hated, she well knew, by her master,—lay
like a dead weight on nurse's heart. Was there a
fate in the daughters of the proud house loving
these farmers? or had Miss Castle had a hand in
bringing the two together?

If any woman disliked another, nurse did Miss
Castle. She read her character truly, and knew
she was artful and designing. As to admitting
her into the sick room, it needed not Sir Cyrus'

mandate, or poor Cynthia's feeble cry of, "Don't let Miss Castle come in;" to induce nurse to shut the door against her. The story of typhus fever and infection had answered well; Miss Castle kept strictly to those rooms furthest removed from Cynthia's, wore camphor bags, filled her room with all kind of disinfecting fluids, and fumigated it two or three times a day, making it smell—so the servants said—"worse than a pigstye!" But secrets—even the closest kept—will out somehow, and nurse had within the last few days detected a mocking smile on Miss Castle's face, as she inquired, half in French, on purpose to annoy nurse, "how her *chére demoiselle* was?" and that nurse looked "*pale comme un ange*," and she was dreadfully afraid she would be the next to take that "*affreux*—typhus."

"I'm not a bit afraid, miss," returned nurse, grimly.

"Ah! is there no fear, then? It is so terribly infectious."

"It is," replied nurse, more severely than

before; "but I've nursed worse cases than this."

"But none so catching?" said she, with so mocking a smile playing about the corners of her lips, that nurse would have gladly turned her back upon her if she could.

"You have been my best friend. You are my *béte noire*," said she, with another mocking smile, as she took both nurse's hands in hers and pressed them. "What should I have done without you to do all the work for me?"

"What work?" asked nurse, stiffly, as she drew her hands away and crossed them determinedly at her waist.

"What work? Ah! you do not like to be thanked. You are meek; you are a *mauvais sujet*. But have you not nursed that dear young lady— that *petite vipère* for me?"

"A *pettet* what?" asked nurse, angrily, half suspecting her French phrases and words were anything but complimentary.

"*Petite*, means little; and *vipère*, angel. I am

so fond of my pupil, so longing to see her again. When is it to be, Nurse Joyce?"

"I don't know. Best ask Mr. Gibbs," and nurse turned on her heel and went back to Cynthia, her temper sadly ruffled—although, if asked, she could not have explained why.

"Was that Miss Castle you were speaking to?" asked Cynthia.

"Yes, Missey; and she's, without exception, the tiresomest woman I ever had any dealings with, giving me a lot of her French talk, which I like as much as I do French rolls. Give me good substantial, home-made bread, and none of your flimsy, light, Frenchified baking, that puff out the inside and don't fill it, bringing on cholics and such like."

"She cannot help her French sometimes, nurse. Her mother was a Frenchwoman, and she has spent half her life in France. Her being such a good French scholar was the reason, I believe, of papa's engaging her."

"Humph!" replied nurse. "I've always heard

the French are a wicked, deceitful set, hugging
up idols, and bowing and scraping to dolls dressed
in tawdry finery. So she's half French, is
she? with all the bad qualities of those heathens,
and none of the good ones of us English. She's
just like a cat; treads about as softly when it
suits her, and hides her claws till the time comes
to make a spring, and then she'll put up her back
and tear and scratch as bad as any of 'em. I'm
not taken in with her palavering or soft velvety
paws either," and nurse angrily wiped with her
apron the hands Miss Castle had so lately held in
hers ; " she'll show me her nails some days, and
sharp one's they'll prove; but they won't wound
me for all that, or if they do, the wound 'll soon
heal. She purrs faster and more insinuating than
a cat down-stairs ; and would curl herself up on
Sir Cyrus' knees and make herself comfortable, if
she only dared. I only hope she'll never be asked
to."

Cynthia laughed one of her old merry ringing
laughs, and then, as though the exertion had been

too much for her, fell to crying the moment after;
while nurse, in utter dismay, and with many self-
upraidings for having talked too much, hung
over her, and tried to soothe and quiet her.

How often nurse sighed day after day as
she watched Cynthia's utter want of energy, or
the sad, weary look on her young face; sighed and
wished she would only open her heart to somebody; tell the sorrowful tale, the weight of which
lay crushing her heart so terribly, that before long
it might break; and now a few light words
spoken hastily, almost angrily, had touched
and opened its floodgates.

Throwing her arms round nurse's neck,
Cynthia sobbed out,

"I am so unhappy, Nursey!"

"I know it, my lamb—your old Nursey has
known it for ever so long. Didn't you talk and
moan about it when you were ill. There, stop
crying, which never does any good," said nurse,
soothingly, "and tell me how I can help
you?"

"Papa says I must give him up. And it's that—that—that is breaking my heart."

"And so you will give him up, and think no more about him, my darling, when Sir Cyrus brings some fine handsome young man to see you. Ah! you should have seen the noble-looking gentlemen that came courting your lady mother; such a lot of them, too; and many richer and braver looking than Sir Cyrus."

"But I cannot give him up, Nursey—I cannot."

"But he isn't so well born as you, nothing like it; nor no money neither, and you'd may be starve—and he wouldn't thank you, or love you for that, I know."

"He will work for me, and so will I for him."

"What could you do, my pet?" and nurse stroked and fondled the small white hands. "These," she said, "are too daintily made for work; and as for him— Well, I dare say he could work fast enough, although he hasn't shown much heart for it yet. All the same, work or no work, an Alywin is not the one you should mate with."

" Don't say that, Nursey," and Cynthia hid her face on nurse's shoulder, as the rich blood dyed it crimson at the mention of her lover's name.

"I can't say nothing else—I can't think nothing else. It's a sorrowful beginning, and, if persisted in, will be a more sorrowful ending. I puzzle myself to find out however you came across him. But, there, I suppose it was Miss Castle's doing."

" Miss Castle !" cried Cynthia, indignantly, while her eyes flashed, and something of the old proud expression came for a moment across her face ; " she does not know him. He hates her as much as I do."

" I honour him for that," replied nurse. " But, my darling, listen to your old Nursey, who loves you with all her heart, and believe her when she says that no good—only harm—direful harm can

ever come of your love for an Alywin. Look at
your aunt! Didn't she, poor lady, waste her life
for one of them, and didn't he snap his fingers at
her, and marry a linendraper's daughter? People
did say his father worried him into it; but was
your aunt worried into a marriage with the earl,
for all the terrible life old Sir Cyrus led her?
Give him up, darling; try and forget him for
my sake."

"Never! Nursey."

"When it will bring us all such misery, such
sorrow? And, most of all, to you, Missey," said
she, pleadingly.

"Sorrow! misery! There can be none where
he is, or if there was, I would gladly share it
with him," and Cynthia's lip curled with anger,
defiance, and strong determination.

"Don't be angry, Missey, don't. Only give
him up; not all at once; no, I don't ask that,
but by degrees, and I'll bless you as long as I
live."

"I will never desert him!" replied Cynthia,

raising herself up on the sofa. "I see how it is, you as well as papa would do him harm if you could. But I will rouse myself. I will get well. I will go and tell him. No one shall make me cease to love him—I will die rather. As long as he loves me, I will love him—I swear I will!" and, overcome with the unwonted exertion, Cynthia lay back, fainting.

Nurse wrung her hands, and flew here and there for restoratives.

"Deary me!" cried she, as the tears fell from her eyes, "to think that after all my care my precious lamb should be brought to this pass!" and she chafed Cynthia's hands, raised her head, and busied herself afresh to restore animation.

It was not a long faint; perhaps Cynthia's strong will conquered it, or the violent beatings of her heart strove against it; but whatever it was, she soon opened her eyes, and, seeing nurse's pitying face, she nestled herself close in her arms, like a tired child, and said, pleadingly,

"You will not turn against me, Nursey, will you?"

"I'll go through fire and water to serve you first. Forget what your old Nursey said, darling, and tell me how I can help you."

"You *will* help me, nurse?" asked Cynthia, doubtingly.

"I will. And if I am doing wrong, may God forgive me!" said she, with a sigh.

"Nursey," replied Cynthia, and she drew her closer still, "dear Nursey, you will go and see how *he* is, and where he is; for I cannot rest, until I know that he is safe and—and unhurt," and she covered her face with her hands, as she thought of the terrible scene by the water's edge. "Oh, Nursey, if you only knew why I am so anxious—if you only knew why."

"Hush! my darling, hush! I'll find it all out for you; I'll go now—I'll go at once; and may God forgive me for going!" said she, aside; "for I know I am doing wrong. I know nothing but misery can come of it."

As she opened the door to pass out, Sir Cyrus stood on the threshold.

"How is your young mistress?" he asked.

"She's better, Sir Cyrus. But if you want to see her well, put a little life into the old house. If you want to get rid of an old fancy, you can't do it without bringing about a fancy for something else. The old song says, 'Best to be off with the old love before you are on with the new.' But Miss Cynthia has nothing new to take on with, so she clings to the old. It's the heart with her ; not the body, that ails now."

Sir Cyrus went on into his daughter's room to find her, as nurse had said, looking better ; her cheeks flushed, and her eyes brighter than they had been for days.

CHAPTER XI.

RAYMOND.

" Put a little life into the old house." These words of nurse's haunted Sir Cyrus. Life ! must the sounds of song and merriment once more echo through the old walls?—sounds that for sixteen years he and they had been strangers to. Sixteen years ! Had so long a time elapsed since he had been left desolate, and she, his wife, so passionately loved, snatched from him in the bloom of her youth and beauty ? Ah ! it needed not that white tablet with the weeping angels, under

which he sat every Sunday at church, to remind
him that she had died, at the early age of twenty-
seven, for had not his heart been desolate, his
life a weary one, for sixteen years? And now,
to break its repose, call it into activity again,
seemed like a desecration of the dead, an insult
to the memory of her who still held the first
place there.

To him it seemed but as yesterday that she had
been borne away and buried from his sight, so
fresh in his heart was the recollection of that terrible time, when all his hopes, his love, had become as a thing that was, and would never
gladden his sight again; and now, to put a little
life into the old house—tear out—root up all
his old feelings and associations, unmanned
him completely. The sense of what he for his
daughter's sake was called upon—might have—to
do, rested like a dead weight on his heart for days,
until it shaped itself into words, and then acts.

Sir Cyrus was not a man to procrastinate or
put off for to-morrow what might be done to-

day; sufficient was it to him that it must be done to do it at once, and he began by inviting, not the small world round about his estate, but his nephew, the heir to Stonycleft.

Sir Cyrus had never seen his nephew, never heard of or from him; but he knew that such a man existed, who only waited for his death to step in and take possession. He might be a spendthrift, a gambler, a drunkard; save that such a character or characters had seldom stained the escutcheon of the proud house of Bedfield. He was his brother's only son—only child, in fact, born in Australia, where that brother had emigrated shortly after his marriage with his wife. How well he remembered that wife; proud, haughty, and beautiful, whom old Sir Cyrus, his father, hated long before he saw her, simply because she was poor and low-connected in comparison with his aristocratic brother. She was looked upon as an interloper, an intriguer, who had angled for his brother when a young man at Oxford, and won him. What wonder that storms and unhappiness, and constant bickerings, if not

quarrels, were the result of her domicile under
her father-in-law's roof; or that old Sir Cyrus,
in a sudden fit of fury, should have at last shut the
door in his son's face, with an oath that he would
never see him again. That oath his son
helped him to keep by emigrating to Australia,
where only a death-bed forgiveness could reach
him, and did reach him before he died ; not pen-
niless, but a wealthy sheep farmer, leaving one
son, whom his UNCLE now wished to see, not
only his guest, but Cynthia's husband.

Sir Cyrus had shared in his father's dislike of
his brother's wife, and unconsciously hoped that
she no longer existed ; at all events, his igno-
rance in the matter would prevent his including
her in his invitation to her son, to whom he thus
wrote :

"Stonycleft.

"MY DEAR SIR,

"As the only male representative
of our ancient family, and its future heir, I write
to invite you to Stonycleft, as it is but right you

should be introduced to possessions, which, in all probability you will soon have to take the charge of. It will give me much pleasure to welcome you here, as also to become acquainted with my brother's son. My daughter, who is only just recovering from severe illness, unites with me in kindest regards.

" Your affectionate uncle,

" CYRUS BEDFIELD."

This letter cost Sir Cyrus a good deal of trouble, and even when finished and despatched, he felt dissatisfied with it. He sent it, enclosed to his solicitors, not knowing his nephew's address.

The reply was short and concise, and, Sir Cyrus thought, off-hand. It certainly did not appear to have cost the writer a thought as to how it should be worded, or what he should say, but was dashed off in a free-and-easy sort of style, and stated, in a few words, that the writer would be at Stony-cleft in a week. No day, no date was fixed, so

that Sir Cyrus was—although he would not
acknowledge it to himself—in a constant state of
fever and anxiety.

But the week passed, and brought no signs of
his nephew. It wanted but two days to the fort-
night, and the baronet, who looked upon unpunctuality as a heinous sin, began to change the
favourable opinion he had almost unconsciously
predisposed himself to take of his nephew, Miss
Castle cunningly helping to influence his mind
against him whenever she could, and as Sir
Cyrus often spoke of him, her opportunities were
frequent.

She had wormed herself completely into Sir
Cyrus' favour, or, as nurse had said, purred
herself into it, and if as yet she had not been
bold enough to curl herself up on his lap, she was
advancing very rapidly towards that enviable
position.

The nephew's invitation, although not exactly
a death blow, was a knell for the present to her
hopes. She reasoned that while he was at Stony-

cleft her interests would be extinguished ; there-
ore she hated him before he came, and determined, if possible, to prejudice Sir Cyrus against
him. If Cynthia married him, Sir Cyrus, for his
daughter's sake, would never take a wife. If
Cynthia did not marry him, or he refuse to
marry Cynthia, Sir Cyrus, out of revenge, might
take a second wife; and if he did, might she not
induce him to choose her? Her father had been
a General, whatever her mother's antecedents
were, and these latter she felt must not be
enquired into too closely. As yet she had played
her cards well, and why not play a trump card
and win ? Had not that vulgar Mrs. Alywin
said *she* would be " my lady " in a year if she
only had the run of the house?

Miss Castle drew up her head proudly, as she
whispered, " My lady," comporting herself for
the moment, as though she already had the right
and title to be called so.

Miss Castle sat in the drawing-room,—from
which Cynthia had just been moved away up-

stairs, for she was still scarcely strong enough to remain for any length of time below,—and gazed round at the costly ornaments scattered about, and the beautiful paintings that adorned the walls. Amongst the latter, a full length portrait of the late Lady Bedfield stood conspicuous, a portrait that Miss Castle had, at first, regarded with envy, and latterly with absolute loathing and dislike. It represented a fair, very beautiful girl, almost too delicate and fairy-looking for the heavy, rich folds of white satin that fell around her light, graceful form. Her eyes were as blue and liquid-looking as the unclouded sky above her head, eyes so soft and melting that they seemed to claim the gazer's love and sympathy, with a depth of feeling in them that might light them up with the fire of scorn and indignation as well as love. They were eyes from which there was no escape. They haunted and followed you wherever you went, and Miss Castle turned her back upon them as she sat, then suddenly rose and faced them angrily.

" Beautiful !—lovely !—bewitching !—fascinating !—" exclaimed she, with a pause between each word. " These are only a few of the admiring terms I have had the pleasure of silently hearing lavished on you and your eyes ; eyes that I hate and mock at. *Bah!* What harm can they do me ? Their day is nearly over, and I will dethrone you, lovely and fascinating one. You shall come down from that high altar where you have been perched for sixteen years and more, and I, the magnificent, will reign there instead. You may mock me with that perpetual smile, but I swear it! I swear it! and will never forget my oath. Never!" and she shook her finger savagely at the lovely portrait, which even now appeared to smile at her more mockingly than ever.

" What ! Do you swear, fair lady ?" asked Sir Cyrus, banteringly, as he advanced to her side ; " and what is the nature of your oath ?"

He had heard a part of her angry tira le, but very fortunately for her, *not all.*

For a moment Miss Castle thought her cause lost. She turned, with a defiant expression on her handsome face; then, the lines about her mouth relaxed, the lips parted, and a soft smile rested on them, lighting up her large grey eyes, which drooped bashfully before Sir Cyrus' steady gaze. She had recovered her presence of mind by her strong power of will, and almost hated herself for the momentary weakness which had nearly betrayed her.

" We swear at anything in France," replied she, carelessly, and with only the very slightest tremor of voice; " but I was repeating Colonel Knollys' words. You know I was in the room when he called yesterday."

As Sir Cyrus looked enquiringly at her, she felt obliged to tread deeper in the mire, in which she was already struggling helplessly.

" It was in allusion to Lady Cyrus' portrait," she said. " He swore it was the most beautiful he had ever seen."

The smile faded from Sir Cyrus's face. He

turned away without raising his eyes, and taking
up a book, effectually hid his face from Miss
Castle, giving her plainly to understand that he
desired to be alone, a hint she was not slow to
take.

Miss Castle would have been a masculine
woman, as her height and—sometimes—bearing
betokened, but for the subjection, the constant check she kept on all her acts and movements, it being her study and aim to be
thought a weak, dependant one. She was always
impressing on the baronet, in hints cleverly
mixed up in their conversation, how she longed
to have as a friend, some one with a firm strong
will on which to lean her weak one. Nevertheless, she was often inadvertently guilty of little
acts that showed at once the strength and masculine tendency of her mind. In the present instance she crushed the *heel* of her boot somewhat
roughly on the ground, and once more bent her
brow angrily and fiercely at the ever smiling por-

trait.   Had she been a man she would have cursed her thoughtless folly in not being more cautious ; being a woman, she was contented with calling herself opprobrious names.

" I'm a fool !" muttered she, bitterly, as she went out of the room ; "a fool! with only a fool's wit and discretion.   My mother would never have been so surprised or nearly caught, *Toujours gai*—always gay ; *toujours souriante*—always smiling.   These four words were all she had to bequeath me on her death-bed.   Nevertheless they made her fortune *once*, although she was not wise enough to keep it ; and she said they would make mine.   How nearly I was forgetting them but now.   It is so hard to smile when one's heart is beating with passion ; angry passion, or fear.   I will never act on the defensive again ; never be betrayed into it; it shall be a deliberate act into which I must be forced," and with a smile on her handsome face she almost danced up stairs, humming, " *Toujours gai—toujours souriante.*"

But her song was suddenly hushed by the violent ringing of the hall bell. It was not merely
a quick ring, but a loud prolonged peal.

"At this hour!" cried she, as going close to
the painted windows she looked at her watch;
"nearly seven o'clock, who can it be?" she
hesitated, and then suddenly making up her mind
for action, fled as quick as thought down the stairs
again, and into the room she had just quitted.

Sir Cyrus had laid down his book, and with
his elbows resting on the table, had shaded his
face with his hands.

It was not a propitious moment for Miss Castle.
At any other time she would not have dared
disturb him, but would have retreated softly.
She was an expert tactician, and knew at a glance
how ill-timed her presence must be, when his
whole attitude bespoke grief; but she had an
excuse, a grand excuse for disturbing his thoughts,
filled, she well knew, with mournful remem-
brances of his lost wife; and it was with a plea-
surable, almost savage feeling, she advanced and

I 5

laid her hand gently on his arm, but the tones of her voice were soft and meek, belying the angry, scornful flash of her eyes.

"Sir Cyrus," she whispered, "Sir Cyrus!"

But she was quite unprepared for the angry way in which he shook off her hand, and sprung to his feet.

"Madam!" he exclaimed, drawing up his figure to its full height, "you forgot yourself strangely. You presume too much."

How her heart beat with indignation and wounded pride; but she was not to be caught twice, and was in no wise daunted at having angered Sir Cyrus. She felt no fear as she clasped her white, shapely hands together, and looked beseechingly in his face; a becoming attitude that had disarmed his anger once before, and made him pronounce her a handsome woman.

"Oh pray, pray forgive me. I thought you would like to know of your nephew's arrival. I did indeed," said she, tremblingly.

Sir Cyrus' brow relaxed. "Where is he?" he asked.

"I do not know. I have not seen him. I only heard the hall bell ring."

"Your judgment is as hasty as your acts, madam, and most likely the former, as well as the latter, have led you astray. I fancy Mr. Gibbs has not paid his usual visit to day;" these last words were said rather sarcastically.

"Mr. Gibbs!" exclaimed she; "Mr. Gibbs ring like that! Oh, impossible, he has not the nerve for it. It may be Mrs. Alywin," she said, after a moment's thought.

The Baronet looked disconcerted, and involuntarily made a hasty movement towards the door, but he was too late. It was flung wide open by the pompous butler, "Mr. Bedfield," cried he, in a stentorian voice.

A tall—very tall man entered, while Sir Cyrus relieved from his momentary fear of a second attack from his lady friend, advanced and greeted him, more warmly than he otherwise should.

"Welcome, nephew," he said, "welcome to Stonycleft;" and then he introduced Miss Castle, who, with her large eyes fixed on his face, scanned him eagerly, but the light—it was almost dusk—prevented any very successful scrutiny.

"And what kind of a journey have you had?" inquired the baronet; "did you run it in one day?"

"No, sir, I started from town this morning," answered he, carelessly.

Sir Cyrus' brow clouded. There was a silence, and then Sir Cyrus spoke again, but a stiffness was gradually creeping over his manner, while the hearty, cheery voice with which he had greeted his nephew vanished.

"Racketing for ten days, or over head and ears in business. Which?"

"Neither. I was only three days in town."

"Your arrival here has been hourly expected for the last ten days," chimed in Miss Castle, determined to do him an ill turn if she could.

"Did I specify any particular day?" asked he, quite coolly ; "I fancy not."

"In a week's time, sir," exclaimed his uncle, testily; "a week's time from the date of your letter."

"I regret," said Mr. Bedfield, turning to Miss Castle, "that I should seemingly have been guilty of a rudeness; I never supposed my non-arrival would have caused any one the slightest incon- veinence, and least of all to my uncle. A gentle- man's society is always counted as nothing amongst a number of other visitors."

"Number of visitors!" echoed Sir Cyrus. "I have invited no one but yourself. I think I mentioned how seriously ill my daughter has been. Her state of health will of necessity preclude all idea of visitors. You are the first stranger, ahem! visitor," corrected he, "who has set foot in Stonycleft, as a guest, since Lady Bedfield's death," and his voice shook, as it always did at any allusion to his wife; while Miss Castle wondered how he had nerved himself to mention her name at all.

"Shall I ring for lights?" she asked.

" By all means, madam ;" and the rustle of her dress, as she moved to and fro, was the only sound that broke the awkward silence that ensued.

" Devonshire is a lovely country," said Miss Castle, addressing Mr. Bedfield.

" Lovely ! we get none of the cold sharp winds you get here; still, soft and mild as the climate is, a more bracing one would suit my mother better," said he, glancing at his uncle.

Sir Cyrus started.

" I am glad to learn Mrs. Bedfield is well. I feared to touch upon the subject in my letter, so forbore mentioning her name, lest the theme should be a painful one," he forced himself to say.

" Thank you. My mother is wonderfully well; you remember her I dare say.

" Perfectly. Her face was one not easily forgotten."

At this juncture, lights were brought, and again Miss Castle furtively scanned the visitor's face.

Raymond Bedfield was a fine looking man; with a powerful, muscular, well-made frame. He looked as if with those strong arms and hands, he could crush or grind any thing to powder that resisted his will. But he was not a handsome man, in fact he was ugly. He had a florid complexion, and large head, covered with thick masses of hair of the unfortunate Bedfield tint, although nature had in his case rather overstepped her privilege, by stamping it an unmistakable red, unmodified or softened by any dark shades, but shining in all its glory, a bright sandy hue; the only favour she had shown him, was in bestowing, instead of straight, straggling locks, soft natural curls, which clustered about his high broad forehead. His eyes were small, clear, and piercing, and at times somewhat crafty looking. His mouth was large, and showed at the owner's will a row of very white regular teeth. His hands and feet were also large, in fact he was on a large scale altogether, save the one prominent feature of his face—his nose, which was, for so tall and big a man, especially small, but its defect was at first sight scarcely noticed, on account of a very thick moustache, which grew almost fiercely at its base.

Miss Castle was not prepossessed in his favor, yet so intently taken up with her scrutiny, that she failed to notice how her gaze was returned with interest, or how Mr. Bedfield, although talking to his uncle, was every now and then regarding her fixedly. When she did become aware of it, she flushed deeply, and then paled almost as suddenly, while rising hastily, she, with a "good night," to Sir Cyrus, and a graceful bow to his nephew, but without raising her eyes to his face again, swept her ample skirts after her out of sight.

" Who is that lady?" asked Mr. Bedfield, as the door closed.

" My daughter's governess."

Then seeing his nephew made no reply, he added, " A strikingly handsome woman. Don't you think so?"

The answer came slowly.

" Handsome —handsome.   Ah !—handsome," said he, abstractedly.

Sir Cyrus laughed.

" You are not the first man by a good many whose thoughts a pretty woman has sent wool gathering."

Mr. Bedfield echoed his uncle's laugh.

" I wasn't thinking of her beauty," he said, " but she *is* undoubtedly a very handsome wo- man."

Meanwhile Miss Castle's skirt rustled grandly up stairs, down the corridors, and into Cynthia's room.

" He has come ! He is here !" cried she, as she entered.

" Here !" exclaimed Cynthia, starting up.

" Not in this room, you silly child, but below, in the drawing-room."

" And what is he like ?" asked Cynthia, who shared in the general anxiety.

" Like ! ugh ! a monster ! Do you remember

the Ogre in the pantomine last year, with sandy hair and unkempt locks ?"

" Surely not so bad as that ?" said Cynthia.

" The Bedfields are a handsome race," said Nurse.

" Handsome? Why he is the ugliest man I ever saw; without exaggeration, the *very* ugliest."

Cynthia laid back on the sofa with a smile on her face.

" I hope papa will think so, too," she said.

" Something has upset Miss Castle," cried Nurse, as once more the skirt rustled away through the door out of sight.

CHAPTER XII.

SIGNS OF A STORM.

EITHER under the pretence or reality of a bad headache, Cynthia kept her room during the next few days; Sir Cyrus, although constantly urging her appearance below, not liking to insist upon it.

" Your cousin is anxious to make your acquaintance, Cynthia," he said, one morning, "and indeed, I think an exertion should be made. It is scarcely gracious your remaining away so long.

You must make an effort, lest your absence be attributed to discourtesy."

But Miss Castle, who happened to be present, did not second this wish.

" I think Miss Bedfield does wisely," said she; " first impressions are everything, especially with men.   Cynthia's eyes are heavy and swollen, and she can hardly be expected to exert herself when her spirits are so depressed with constant pain."

But Cynthia did not take advantage of this speech; she seemed suddenly to think differently and act differently.

" I will endeavour to come down this evening, papa," said she.

" That's right, my child."

" I am sure it is not a wise step," said Miss Castle.

But her words went for nothing. Nobody heeded them except nurse, who frowned,—or more properly speaking,—scowled at her over her spectacles.

Miss Castle, strange to say, showed no anxiety to commence the hostilities she had promised herself, or even further, publicly, her scrutiny of Mr. Bedfield; otherwise she would have eagerly joined in persuading her pupil to make a move to the drawing-room, as of course, until Cynthia did so, she was of necessity precluded from joining Sir Cyrus and his nephew; so she was compelled to watch matters at a distance, and did so rigorously from every available window, point, or position. For instance, she would take her stand at a front window during such times as Raymond Bedfield might be wandering about the park and wait patiently until he returned, all the time eagerly keeping him in sight, and watching him somewhat in the fashion of an eagle scenting its prey, save that when his foot was on the balustraded terrace and he almost beneath where she stood, she would gradually shrink away out of sight. At other times, hidden behind one of the bear's heads carved at an angle of the large staircase, she would watch him put on his hat and

glove before going out. Once she carried a telescope
up to the parapet that ran along the front of the
house above the rooms she occupied, and eyed
him and Sir Cyrus as they rode away on horse-
back, but her spying seemed unsatisfactory, for
she sighed heavily as she came down from her
post of observation, while a restless, almost
pained look swept over her features and settled
momentarily on her face.   Often, after a close
scrutiny of his tall form from behind a window
curtain she would be lost in thought, from which
she would rouse herself apparently mortified and
disappointed.   Once, after one of these fits of
abstraction, she rose grandly, and almost clenched
her hands as she muttered,

" It is impossible, utterly impossible ! Being
too much alone breeds these nervous fancies."

She was certainly not anxious to meet him
face to face again, otherwise, instead of this covert
espionage, so unworthy of her, what so easy as
to have managed a meeting in the park, where he
o constantly wandered.

As Sir Cyrus rose to leave his daughter, he turned to Miss Castle.

" You will of course chaperone your charge, this evening, Miss Castle. I have not had a good cup of coffee since you ceased to preside at the tea table."

This was true, as Sir Cyrus invariably sweetened it either too much, or, vice versa, too little, and grumbled accordingly.

" Must I come down?" she replied.

- " Must you? Of course you must. Cynthia, silly child, will be nervous at facing her cousin for the first time; besides she requires a chaperon now more than a governess !"

" At what hour will you be ready, Cynthia?" asked Miss Castle, when they were alone.

" Oh ! some time in the evening after dinner; between seven and eight, I suppose."

When Miss Castle reached her room, she—instead of reconnoitring from the window as usual,—sat down by the table, and leaning her head on her hand, was soon lost in one of her lately frequent fits of thought.

"Requires a chaperon more than a governess, now," murmured she, presently, "but for that speech, I would have rebelled against going below while *he* remains; but I cannot help myself. *Coûte que coûte,* I *must*, if I wish ever to reign here. That speech of Sir Cyrus's tells me as plainly as words can, that my *rôle* as a governess is very nearly over. My slave will be emancipated, and must have a chaperon; and if I refuse?—but I cannot refuse. I will meet this man with a *coup de main* and defy him!" and she laughed; but not heartily.

Just then a shrill whistle and a dog's loud bark, sounded from beneath Miss Castle's open window.

Her window was always half open now; she seemed either to have forgotten or to feel little of the chilliness of which she used so frequently to complain to Cynthia, although the days were fast merging into Autumn.

At the sounds she rose hastily but noiselessly, and cautiously approached the window. Mr. Bedfield, with a large whip in one hand, and in the other holding a chain which was attached to Nero's collar, was just starting for a walk; while Sir Cyrus stood on the terrace encouraging and inciting Nero to go with him. But the dog, notwithstanding the Baronet's repeated mandates of, " Go with him, sir! Hie on !" still resisted, and it was not until he had administered a sharp reprimand in the shape of a severe switch across his back with his hunting whip, that Nero sulkily followed or allowed himself to be unwillingly led by Raymond Bedfield.

" The dog hates him as much as he does me," said Miss Castle. " I wish he would tear his throat and leave him a prey for the worms. But there ! there is no such luck."

She drew away from the window and opened the drawers one after the other, pulling out the dresses they contained.

"If I wanted to create a sensation, I should wear this," and she unfolded a pale lavender poplin trimmed with cerise. "It is the most becoming dress I have," and she advanced to the glass and held it before her. It contrasted well with her dark skin and hair; and it was with a sigh she refolded it, and put it back in its place. She turned over the others one by one, examining and commenting on each in turn before putting them by. Then she took a bunch of keys from her pocket and opened a large trunk. It was seemingly filled with dresses. She did not displace them, but kneeling down, lifted them with one hand and diving below with the other, seized hold of one which she dragged out of the box by main force on to the floor.

She lifted it and unfolded a rich black silk, which she spread out on the bed. It seemed,—as it laid there so gloomily with its dark hue in strong contrast with the white counterpane, to have a strange depressing effect upon her; for she clasped her hands round the bed-post, and leaning her forehead against its carving, looked at it dejectedly, almost mournfully.

"*He* could not bear me in it," she murmured, presently. "It was too dark and melancholy for those days. Yes, for those days, but not for these. And yet I was more unhappy then than now. But the remembrance, the remembrance! How can I bear to wear it, and recall *that*, or a time that well-nigh broke my heart."

Her eyes filled with tears, but she did not give way to them, or allow them to flow, otherwise, from the trembling of her lips, a passionate burst would have been the consequence. She simply drooped her forehead on to her hands for a minute, then raised her head, and turning away without looking at the dress again, went and stood over at the window. She stood abstractedly, her eyes fixed on vacancy until Nero's deep bark aroused her, and drew her thoughts away from the past to present scenes, and she looked towards where Mr. Bedfield's tall form could be seen strid-

ing along in the distance, still with the dog unwillingly following him.

" I wonder where he his going with the dog ? I
wonder, I wonder."

Was it a sudden impulse prompted her,—as in
Cynthia's case, when she had dogged her footsteps
by the river,—to snatch her hat and. shawl and
hurry away into the park.

Sir Cyrus was smoking on the terrace, and she
half retreated as she saw him, then boldly
advanced to where he sat.

" A lovely afternoon for a walk," said Sir
Cyrus.

" Yes, but the evenings grow cold," she replied, as she lingered a moment, then passed
him, drawing her shawl rather closer around
her.

" She will soon be warm walking that pace,"
thought Sir Cyrus, as she hastily swept away out
of sight.

Miss Castle hurried on. It was close upon
four o'clock, and she had yet a long way to go,

and must get back in time to dress for the evening.

Down the drive and away to the right, amongst
the brushwood and over the fences she scrambled,
and so on to the hills that overhung the river; but
avoiding their edges; below which she guessed
Mr. Bedfield was walking. Reaching the slope
of the hill she hurried down it into the wood,
following the narrow pathway until she reached
a small open glade, where the trees had been carefully cleared away, and a small wooden seat
erected. Here Miss Castle, fairly out of breath,,
seated herself, but had hardly done so before a
footstep sounded, apparently not so very far away,
while Nero's growl and then bark rang out
through the stillness of the wood, scattering the
sparrows and small birds, whose wings hastily
fluttered about in all directions, ere they winged
their flight.

Miss Castle sprung to her feet, then sat down
again and quickly pulled her veil, which was a
thick one, over her face; but presently as though

a sudden thought struck her, she caught up her dress and crept softly and cautiously between the trees, and in another moment was completely hidden from sight, but not from the dog's scent, who, as Mr. Bedfield advanced to the very spot where Miss Castle had so lately been seated, looked with his bright eyes in the direction where she was crouched, and growled ominously.

Miss Castle trembled excessively. Would Mr. Bedfield loose him? She closed her eyes with fear, and already seemed to feel in imagination his sharp fangs on her throat. Would he,—Oh! would he, let him loose?

No, he would not loose him. The dog's growl had either not been heard, or heard and not understood.

Mr. Bedfield after a moment's thought went up to the largest tree; they were mostly small ones growing round the open space, and tested its strength with one of those strong muscular arms of his. It bent; slightly bent, and that was all. He dragged Nero close to it, and tied him there; the dog, although growling, making no resistance, his attention being attracted to the bush behind which Miss Castle was.

Having secured Nero, Mr. Bedfield shook out the lash of his whip and held it menacingly before the dog; while Miss Castle, with a shudder, noticed that his left hand was bound up in a handkerchief, which was dyed and stained with blood. He held this hand almost close to the dog's face, who growled at it savagely.

" Do you see that? you brute !" he said, with an oath, and then deliberately set to work and thrashed him with all his might.

Nero flew to the length of his chain, and had it broken, small would have been Mr. Bedfield's chance of life. Food for the worms he most certainly would have been; for the dog's blood was up, and little mercy would he have shown.

Miss Castle looked on in terror. If the dog got loose her doom was sealed. Did he not hate her? and had he not scented her out? She could not fly ; her limbs seemed to have lost all power, and refused to aid her, while her fascinated gaze saw the uplifted whip before the sound of the blow thrilled through her nerves, paralysing her strength.

But the chain held firm, and after a while the dog lay prostrate and bleeding. Then Mr. Bedfield unchained and dragged him away through the wood to the water's edge, and laved his mouth.

Miss Castle's nerves had received a severe shock. She remained in her hiding place in an almost fainting state, and it was fully half an hour before she was able to get up and walk tremblingly home.

When she reached her room, she rang the bell.

" Mary," said she, to the maid who answered it, " I do not feel well. Can you get me a glass of wine ?"

" La, miss! you do look bad."

" Yes, I am subject to fainting fits ; but do not say a word to any one ; I shall soon be all right again."

"Oh! what a man to have for an enemy!" said she, as she laid on the bed after drinking the wine, and the warm blood began once more to circulate freely. "What a man! A man? nay, but he is a savage! a barbarian! a cold blooded, revengeful wretch, with a heart like a tiger's; who, if he gets an inkling of my plans with his uncle, will pursue me remorselessly until, like the dog, I am exhausted in the strife, and if not beaten, hunted to death. How can I wage war with him? I, a weak woman," said she, in a hopelessly desponding tone, while she pressed her hands tightly on her temples. "But I am not a weak woman!" exclaimed she, suddenly, with energy; "I was once, but not now— not now. No, I shrink, but I will brave him. He shall not defeat me without a struggle."

Half an hour later, she knocked at Cynthia's door, dressed in the black silk, with not a vestige of colour about it, the trimmings of the body and skirt being black. Her hair—which was

K 5

always waved brushed off her face and tied up
in a knot at the back with a bright coloured
ribbon—was combed down smoothly over her
forehead, on which, as I have said, it grew low,
especially on the left side, so that the parting
was of necessity more to the right, giving at first
sight a strange one-sided look to her face ; while
the ribbon and knot had disappeared, and two
long silky plaits curled round her small head.
She looked frightfully pale, notwithstanding the
delicate rose colour that tinged her cheeks, but
failed in lighting up her eyes, which were hag-
gard and heavy, notwithstanding their daring,
fearless look.

" Good gracious, Miss Castle, how ill you look !"
exclaimed Cynthia.

" Do I ?" replied she, carelessly, as walking to
the cheval glass, she turned herself about before
it; " I do not see much difference, excepting
the new fashion of my hair. How do you like
it ?"

"Like it? Not at all," replied Cynthia, bluntly; "I think you have made quite a figure of yourself."

"Ah! It is well I am not a vain woman, otherwise I should be tempted to pull the whole fabric down and build it up again."

"You would scarcely have time to build it up again, as it is close upon eight o'clock; besides, I envy you the privilege of being able to make a fright of yourself."

"How complimentary you are, Cynthia, when I have been striving for ever so long to set myself off to the best advantage, and thought I had succeeded."

"What! with that dreadful widow's peak so plainly visible on your forehead, which until now you have always hidden so successfully? But please do not let us both go down cross and out of temper," said she, seeing Miss Castle looked a little offended; "it is your fault I have said so much, but what with your hair and black dress— you, who are so fond of gay colours—I declare I should scarcely recognise you, and I am sure papa will not."

Miss Castle smiled quite blandly.

" Not recognise me ?" echoed she.

" No, I should not," said Cynthia, taking her arm, and then adding, as though a sudden thought struck her, "but I suppose you have a motive for disguising yourself, for I can call it nothing else. Or perhaps you think it necessary, now you are no longer my governess but my chaperon, to alter your style, and come out as *une grande dame.*"

Miss Castle bit her lip and made no reply to this impertinent speech ; but oh ! if she ever did indeed become *une grande dame* and step-mother to the little tormentor by her side, how she would make her pay for all her spiteful, wounding speeches.

They entered the drawing-room, where Sir Cyrus and his nephew already were.

" I feared your headache had returned," said the former, "and was about sending to enquire.

My daughter, Mr. Bedfield. Cynthia, your cousin. Miss Castle, I believe you have already been introduced."

The evening did not pass very smoothly.

Sir Cyrus kept up the old-fashioned custom of having the table laid out for tea, and Miss Castle, who of necessity presided at it now Cynthia was unable to do so, effectually screened her face from Mr. Bedfield behind the tea urn. Sir Cyrus helped her in this, by placing his nephew exactly opposite her, and close to the sofa on which his daughter lay.

Cynthia looked pale, but very lovely, notwithstanding the loss of her soft curls. The little lace cap, with its pale blue ribbons, was no disfigurement, but, if anything, heightened her beauty, giving her so youthful an appearance, that, but for the occasional fire in her dark eyes, and the sometimes proud impatient toss of her head, she might have passed for a child. She scarcely opened her lips at first, save to reply in

monosyllables to Raymond, and then her soft,
sweet voice was strangely at variance with his
deep, full toned one.   Mr. Bedfield was seldom
at a loss for conversation, and talked on bravely,
apparently heedless of the short, sometimes
sharp answers he received.   Once he re-arranged
Cynthia's pillows for her before Miss Castle could
reach the spot; but then the latter showed no
great alacrity in her movements, but halted half
way, as Cynthia, with a deep blush, thanked her
cousin for his assistance, and flashed her dark
eyes angrily at Miss Castle, who returned to her
game of backgammon with the baronet.

Later on in the evening, as Sir Cyrus set up
the board for another game, Miss Castle glanced
furtively behind her.

" Is there time?" inquired she.

" Plenty.   They are contented enough, and in
no hurry to separate;" and as if to verify his
words, Cynthia laughed gaily.   " There!" said
he, " did you hear that! You women are strange

beings; a little well timed flattery soon wins
over the most obdurate of you. How soon he,"
and he nodded meaningly at his nephew, " has
thawed the ice."

" He would never win *me* over," she replied,
quietly.

Sir Cyrus laughed.

" Why not ?" he asked.

" Because—you must not be angry ?"

" Angry ! Of course not."

" Then—I do not like Mr. Bedfield."

" That's a blot," said Sir Cyrus, rattling the
dice and preparing for his throw; " now see if I
don't take you up. There ! I have. And made
a point moreover."

Was it the pleasure of getting such an advantage in the game, the anxiety of making a still
better throw, made him hesitate ere he threw
again ? while, leaning forward, he whispered almost in her ear,

" Neither do I. Neither do I," and then the

dice rattled down so fiercely, that Cynthia quite started.

"Dear papa! pray do not do that again. Miss Castle, when you have finished that game, will you ring for the night candles?"

CHAPTER XIII.

MORE CHANGES THAN ONE.

MONEY and interest were, in the days of which I write, two sure stepping-stones to obtaining a commission in the army. Mugging up for examinations was then unheard of; not but what, had the regulations required it, Frederick Alywin might have come off with flying colours, or, at the least, passed a good, if not a first-class examination, for he was not by any manner of means a dull man, but sharp and quick, if not clever. During his college life, although extravagant, he was not recklessly so. His mother said his being there cost a sight of money; but his debts were mostly incurred in keeping up appearances, or, as he explained it, cutting a dash like any other fellow. Fred, to do him justice, had studied hard and well, and would have passed his "little go" with ease, had not the lash of Sir Cyrus's whip thrashed out all desire of entering the Church; for, if he did, how and where would be his revenge?—which still burnt fiercely in his heart, clogging all its best feelings.

It was in November—dreary, dull November, Fred found himself gazetted as ensign in one of Her Majesty's regiments of the line, under orders to sail for India, and he to join forthwith. Sir Cyrus had managed his part of the business successfully, and, so far as he was concerned, well; but Frederick Alywin laughed in his sleeve at the trick, and saw through it more easily than Sir Cyrus imagined.

What bustle and confusion in the little house at Broadbelt, as the days drew on for Fred's departure! What tearful, sad eyes from Charlotte! What hysterical sobs and abuse of Sir Cyrus from Mrs. Alywin!

The latter had been to Stonycleft, in the first moments of her despair; had begged and beseeched—had implored with all a mother's fears and griefs; but all in vain. Her blandest smiles, her tears and sobs were fruitless,—the baronet was impervious to all, even to flattery, and would do nothing in the matter, or help her if he could. The Horse Guards—of which she knew as much as she did of Greek or Latin— were to blame, not he; and as to giving her a letter to some great personage about Court, who would help her to petition the Queen, the idea convulsed Sir Cyrus with laughter, and much irritated and scandalised Mrs. Alywin; who went home to her bed, and there cried to her heart's content and relief, until she was tired, or had no more tears to shed, when she got up and busied herself—with doleful sighs—in helping pack her scn's things.

"I shall never see the half of these clothes again," said she, dotting down a list of the several articles Charlotte was collecting together for one of the trunks. "However is a young man to look after eight dozen pocket handkerchiefs ! he'll use each of them once, and then they'll be thrown about and lost or stolen—six dozen shirts, ditto socks." (Mrs. Alywin, who, as I have said, had been in the linen drapery business, spelt them *sox*). "Only fancy the holes we shall have to mend ! large enough to put one's thumb through, I'll be bound; while as to the shirts, he'll most likely come home without a rag to his back !"

"I hope he will not remain abroad so long as that," sighed Charlotte, mournfully.

"I wish to goodness, girl, you'd not talk in that tone. I'm heart-broken enough already, without your croaking."

"But when do you think Fred will return, aunt ?"

"When do I think ? why the day after he

goes, if he does go. I'm always hoping something will turn up to prevent him. I don't give
way to the dismals, like you. Why, every time I
hear the postman's knock, I'm fit to jump out of
my skin, thinking it will most likely bring us
good news."

"But, aunt, who could stop Fred's going
now?"

"There you go again! how do I know? But
I do know, 'there's many a slip between the cup
and the lip.' If Fred had only stuck—as he
ought to have done—like a leech to the Church,
all these heart-aches wouldn't have happened.
If—if, if's and and's were—but, there, I mustn't
quote that; Fred says its a vulgar saying, but it
was never thought so in my day. I suppose the
world is getting more polite and particular than
it used to be."

"Shall I pack Fred's regimentals, or do you
think he would rather do so himself?"

"Leave them to the last. Looking at them
helps to console me a little;" and she glanced at

the bright scarlet coat, thrown over the back of
a chair. " It's a lovely, rich-looking stuff, isn't
it? If it had been a dark colour, I could not
have borne it; but I do love the scarlet, it looks
so grand—and Fred looks as handsome as a king
in it. I only wish he'd have worn the whole
toggery at church, yesterday; how I should have
gloried to have heard his sword clattering down the
aisle. The dragoons, at St. Peter's Church, at
Cumber, when I was young, used to make many
a girl's heart dance, with the noise of their spurs
and swords."

" Hark! there's the postman on the opposite
side," said Charlotte, who, unconsciously to herself, shared her aunt's idea of good news.

" Is there? Run down and see for the letters.
It only wants three days now; and if a reprieve
should come, I think I should go out of my
senses."

But no; no reprieve had come; it was only a
letter for Fred.

" Is it a long envelope, with a big splash of

wax for a seal? Those are what Fred calls officials, and all we have to hope for now," sighed Mrs. Alywin.

" There is no seal at all."

" What, wide open?"

" No, aunt; it is gummed down. I will fetch it."

Back Charlotte came with the letter, which she handed to Mrs. Alywin.

" It is a lady's handwriting," said she, her quick eye readily following the dictates of her jealous heart.

" A lady's handwriting! How do you know that?" and Mrs. Alywin took the letter and examined it closely.

It was a small letter—almost a note, and looked smaller than it really was, grasped so rudely in those fat hands, which seemed as though they would crush its sides. The direction was beautifully written in a delicate, running-hand.

" It *is* a lady's writing; and, moreover, it's posted at Broadbelt. I wonder whoever it can

be from?" said Mrs. Alywin, turning and twist-
ing it about; but as she laid it down, she
suddenly bethought her of Miss Castle.

She seized the note again, and re-examined
it.

What could Miss Castle have to say to her
son? Had Sir Cyrus proved too tough for her,
and was she now trying her fascinations elsewhere?

"I am glad he's off, that I am!" exclaimed
Mrs. Alywin, forgetting all about Charlotte, who
looked half frightened—almost scared, at her
aunt's words.

"There, don't stare at me as if I was mad, but
go on with your packing, while I go down and
make a tart for Fred, about the last I shall make
for him."

"Yes, aunt. Shall I give him the letter when
he comes home?"

"Yes—no. It's in my pocket."

Mrs. Alywin fidgetted about the room for a
while, and then, as if suddenly making up her

mind, turned short round and faced the young girl.

" Charlotte! I should like to open this letter.

" Oh, aunt, pray don't!"

" As a mother, mind—as Fred's mother, I have a right to see he is not imposed upon by an artful, designing hussy!—a bold, conceited jade!"

" But—"

" But! But I tell you I've a right to; but I shan't, because you would never see the sense of it where Fred's concerned. Because it's his letter, you'd think me dishonest and sly ;" and in a rage, Mrs. Alywin flung the letter on to the chest of drawers near where Charlotte stood, and flounced out of the room angrily. " I might have talked till doomsday, and never have convinced her !" said she.

Charlotte went on with her packing, until interrupted by Fred.

" Where's the letter mother is making such a fuss about?" he asked.

He read it with a bright flush of pleasure on his face, which did not escape Charlotte's observation.

" Who is Miss Castle?" asked he, presently.

" Miss Bedfield's governess."

He laughed heartily. " I thought as much," he said, " only I fancied there might possibly be two of the same name. Rather a rich idea, that, of my mother's."

" What?" asked Charlotte.

" Didn't she tell you ?" and he laughed again.

" No."

" Well, I half gave you the credit of having put it into her head."

" I never make mischief, as you well know."

" Then I wonder what in the world induced her to make such an absurd guess about the letter being from Miss Castle."   .

" Is it not from her, then ?"

" Of course not. Don't pack those things, Charlotte, give them here. A woman never can fold a coat properly. Why on earth," said he, spreading them on the bed, " does not Jane help you? It's a shame you should have so much trouble on my account."

" I like it," she replied, quietly.

" It's very certain no one would do it as well. I wonder who I shall get to mend my gloves and sew on my shirt buttons by-and-bye. I shall miss you greatly, Charlotte."

" Will you?"

He looked at her in surprise. "What on earth is the matter with you?"

" Nothing, Fred."

" Nothing! Then I wish to Heaven you would talk in a little livelier strain, and not snap a fellow up so."

Fred's sharp reproof wounded her to the quick. It was the second time that day she had been s colded for being low spirited; and utterly subdued and overcome, Charlotte dropped the things she held in her hand, and sitting down on one of the trunks, burst into tears.

Fred's anger vanished. He went hastily towards her.

" Have I said anything to wound you, Charlotte?"

" No, no," she sobbed.

" Then for God's sake don't cry so. What can I say to soothe you? Tell me."

How could she tell him she loved him with all her heart, and that a sharp word from him was more than she could bear? while a kind one was worth all the world beside.

He took her trembling hand in his warm steady ones.

" Charlotte!" he said, " there's no one in the wide world I would sooner have for my wife than you. You would make a different man of me. God knows what I shall be without you!"

The hand he held trembled perceptibly now. He went on.

" And more than that. I believe that even now, *if* I could forego the life I have marked out for myself, I should be, with you by my side, a happier man in the end."

" What life ?" she asked.

" A life that I dare not tell you of. You would trample your love under your small foot; crush it! tear it out of your heart; for I know you love me, Charlotte; and I know with your pure, high-minded notions you would never stand firm, or keep faith with a bad man; and such, one of these days, you will learn to think me."

" Oh, Fred! don't say that. Have I cast you off because you told me that dreadful secret about —about giving up the Church ?"

" No; but you shrank from me for days afterwards."

" Alas, Fred! Can you not understand how grievous your falling away from the truth was to me ?"

" It was the crumbling of the first stone from off the pedestal you had erected in my honour."

" Ah! you acknowledge that ?" she said.

" I acknowledge nothing. The turning Romanist, if I do turn," said Fred, carelessly, "is but a small sin in comparison to those that *must* follow."

"*Must!* There is no must, Fred; no *necessity* for sin, surely?"

"I thought so once; but circumstances alter opinions; at least-they do in my case."

"Oh, Fred! what a way you talk. Does breaking your mother's heart go for nothing?—breaking mine—?"

"It would never break my mother's heart. She, who used to be all love for everybody, now hates Sir Cyrus more bitterly than my brother does. See how *she* has changed; and why should not I? But you—your heart? If anything could turn me from my purpose the breaking that would. Charlotte! I wish to God I had married you a year ago; *now* the thing is impossible, cannot be; nay, more, when I see you again you will no longer love me, possibly have married another."

"And you can talk of it so coolly as this?" asked she, reproachfully.

" We can never be man and wife, although I know you would marry me to-morrow, and think it no sacrifice to be buried alive in this beastly place I'm bound to," said he, with an oath, that startled her, "yet I can't take you there; can't accept your love. It is, perhaps, best for both of us. When I do marry, I shall marry for money, rank, and all the rest of it. Forgive me, Charlotte. I fear I wound you, but I tell you all this for your good. It's very painful to me."

" No you do not!" she said, snatching her hand from his, and confronting him with flaming cheeks; " you tell it to wound and insult me, or if you do not, it *is* an insult! and a gross one. Love you!" continued she, scornfully ; " well, if I do it will not be for long. A Romanist ! perhaps a—a murderer; for how do I know what you are hinting at so darkly? No, you are truly not worth any honest girl's love ; but there is such a word as *remorse!* and that—mark my words—

whatever the sin you contemplate, will haunt you like a fierce fire one of these days."

"I have been driven to it—driven to it," said he, gloomily, as she went away, closing the door rather sharply behind her.

When the evening had closed in Frederick Alywin left the house, and once more struck across the fields towards Stonycleft.

ɤ

CHAPTER XIV.

CAUGHT NAPPING.

Two months have slipped by since the evening
of Cynthia's introduction to her cousin, and we
come to November, with its fogs, short days,
stripped trees, and drizzling rain. Raymond
Bedfield was still a visitor at Stonycleft. With
some who had been prejudiced against him he had
made his peace; with others, his uncle in particular, he had lost ground. Sir Cyrus could not
overcome the dislike he had conceived towards

him, a dislike that increased daily, and was fostered and encouraged by Miss Castle, who on her part viewed him with distrust. That she had a difficult part to play cannot be denied, looked on—as she well knew she was—with suspicion by Mr. Bedfield, she yet managed to steer safely, though at times with imminent risk, among the rocks and shoals in her way. That a quicksand lay ahead into which, by an inadvertent step, she might be plunged and wrecked, she well knew; neither did Mr. Bedfield allow her to forget it. He was always throwing out hints or inuendoes that made her heart quake, although the voice, when she replied, or was forced to parry his attacks, never quavered; it was steady enough.

Perhaps a letter, written by Mr. Bedfield to his mother about this time, will throw a better insight into the state of things at Stonycleft just now, than I can possibly describe.

After tender enquiries as to her health, which had been again ailing, he wrote:—

"I cannot say that I dislike Miss Castle; there my dear Mother you misunderstand me. I admire her too much as yet, to dislike her. I cannot better describe my feelings than by quoting the old distich,

> ' The reason why I cannot tell,
> I do not like you, Mr. Fell.'

That expresses what I feel, capitally. The reason why, has escaped me as yet. Sometimes I lose sight of it altogether; at other times it strikes me forcibly that I have seen her at some prior time. But where? and how? and when? My little cousin, who I promised you I would hate with all my heart, and which promise, by-the-bye, I have only half kept, told me yesterday that the 'chaperon'—she is no longer governess — made a fright of herself as soon as I arrived here. *That* in itself is suspicious, and looks like an attempt at disguise; in fact Cynthia spoke of it as such. I keep my eyes open and my mouth shut as yet, for I have nothing to tax her with; all is dark. I suspect she is playing a deep game

with the baronet, and if my suspicions become certainty, then war to the knife; and you,
my dear mother, must come and help me. Your
wits and memory may be better than mine, unless—which is likely—I may have seen her during
those rambles I took half over the world a year
ago; but for those, I could draw our knowledge of
one another within a very small compass; but in
hunting down a woman a man's not the very best
hand. Woman against woman all the world over.
No compunction, no twitchings of conscience
deters a woman from tabooing another. Give
her a little piece of thread to lay hold of between
her small fingers, and the cotton is unwound to
the very end, and the reel laid bare. I don't
blame your sex; not I. Am I not as vengefully
inclined towards Sir Cyrus, and won't I make
him smart, if I can, for all he made you suffer
Hunt down the chaperon, mother, if you like,
and I swear I'll never lift a finger to help her.
She interests me all the same, and is a study.
Never at fault, never angry, save with her eyes;

do and say what I will. As to the photo detection, she is too crafty for us there, and I find has never had one taken ; so unless we can take her napping—which is unlikely—there is an end to that scheme. But I am ready to try anything else short of murder. I don't blame her for trying to catch the baronet, not I ; but if she marries him there will be the devil to pay, for as sure as fate there will be an heir. Now don't worry and fret about it ; she plays her cards secretly and well, but you and I must try and play ours better. She is a handsome woman, and as crafty as a fox !"

It will be seen from this that the uncle and nephew's dislike was mutual, although the baronet was too polished a gentleman to be uncivil to his guest. His manner was stiff and formal, and without being affable, polite, almost too much so, as in avoiding one evil he ran in danger of the opposite extreme.

Cynthia's spirits had flagged terribly of late.

She was out of the doctor's hands now, and almost herself again, and being emancipated from the school-room she and her cousin were of necessity thrown much together, and were almost on the footing of brother and sister. She was no longer an invalid, although she looked anything but strong; her fair, transparent complexion helping to make her appear more delicate than she really was. She was all anxiety to be out and about the park again, but Sir Cyrus, who lately had taken the greatest care of her, generally decided that the day was either too damp or too cold; or if the sun did shine out, and he, forced to allow that there was no tangible excuse for keeping her within doors, either took her for a drive himself, or Miss Castle accompanied her for a walk. Cynthia grew to know that she was never allowed out by herself, and her spirit rose rebelliously at the surveillance in which she was kept, and as the days drew on for Frederick Alywin's departure her smiles were few and far between, and her whole bearing one of drooping depression, while the baronet's vigilance was, if anything, redoubled tenfold.

Cynthia was a prisoner, and she felt it; while not only her spirit, but her will,—which was as determined as her father's,—rose to fever heat. She knew Sir Cyrus was bent upon preventing a meeting between herself and Frederick Alywin, a meeting she had determined should be; while nurse having exhausted all her arguments passively allowed things to take their course, although with expressed fears and presentiments of the evils that would be sure to arise out of so wilful a course, evils that her young mistress could not and would not see.

Cynthia was dressing for dinner, no very tedious task, now that she had no plaits or hair to arrange, but simply the brush to pass through the soft fair curls. Her face was flushed; she seemed nervous and excitable; one moment depressed, and the next laughing hysterically.

" He,"—Cynthia rarely mentioned Frederick

Alywin by name,—" must have had the letter by this time, nurse ?"

"I put it in the post myself," was the answer, " Miss Castle couldn't have got hold of it, although she did stick to me as long as she could, and tried to ferret out where I was going ; but I can be as deep as she is any day, and unless Miss Castle laid her finger on it after I dropped it in the box, I'm afraid Mr. Alywin,—bad luck to him,"—said she, in a whisper, " has read it long before now."

" You're bent on this work, missy ?" asked she, sorrowfully, as Cynthia turned to leave the room. " Can your old nurse say nothing to turn you from it ?"

" Oh, Nursey ! I thought we had settled all that yesterday. My word is passed, and when did you know me break troth? You only say it to vex me, you dear old tormenting creature."

" Well-a-day ! it's a bad sign when—"

" Don't tell me anything about signs, and

dreams, and omens, and all the rest of it. I don't believe in them, Nursey, and—there," said she, breaking off, "don't look so frightened. I love you with all my heart, that I do," and she threw her arms round the old woman's neck; "but if—if he went away without my seeing him, I should die!" and then, by dint of tears and caresses, Cynthia carried her point, as she always did.

"I shall be back again as soon as dinner is over, or as quickly as I possibly can; so dear—dear Nursey, have everything ready, if you do not wish me to do something more desperate than this moonlight walk you are croaking about."

"And she would," said nurse, when left to herself; "would go off with him perhaps. The Bedfields are a wilful and desperate lot when thwarted; so it's all for the best—all for the best;" but nurse did not think so, for she sighed and muttered to herself again and again.

She was at the wardrobe with Cynthia's seal

skin coat in her hand, when Miss Castle looked in.

"Where is Miss Bedfield?" she asked.

Nurse was startled, and for the moment confused.

" Gone down to dinner, miss," she answered ; and then deliberately turned her back and pulled out one by one, sundry more wraps; shawls and cloaks falling one after another on to the floor.

" What are you doing there?" asked Miss Castle, who had seen her confusion with surprise, and immediately was on the alert.

But nurse had recovered her presence of mind.

" What should I be doing but tidying Miss Bedfield's wardrobe. Do you think I'm going to eat the things?" asked she, impertinently and angrily.

" *Bête !*" exclaimed Miss Castle, stamping her foot, and going down stairs with a still less polite expression,—if not expressed—hovering on her tongue.

" Cousin," said Cynthia, laying her hand on

Raymond's arm as they went into dinner ; " will you do me a favour ?"

" I will."

" With no questions as to the why or where-fore ?"

" With none."

" Then please keep papa as long as you can over his wine to-day."

" Is that all ?"

" All. You promise ?"

" I do," said he, readily ; but Cynthia's eager excited face and earnest manner haunted him all through dinner, and although he asked no ques-tions openly, yet inwardly he was continually trying to solve the why and wherefore.

Miss Castle often took a nap after dinner; latterly this had almost become a confirmed habit ; perhaps it was thus she recruited her strength for the constant sparring and inward war—for it was not an acknowledged one—between herself and Raymond ; certainly she always awoke, looking bright, fresh, and animated—almost defiant. To-night she was more than usually drowsy, Cynthia having sat chatting with her in her room the night before until long past midnight; and no sooner did she find herself on the soft luxuriant sofa, than she fell asleep.

Cynthia rose softly, and as quick as thought was in her own room, where stood nurse with shawl and bonnet on, the tears streaming down her face.

"Quick! quick, nurse!" she cried.

But for all answer the woman dropped on her knees, and with prayers and entreaties sought to dissuade her young mistress, as she had done once before that day.

"Don't, don't be so wilful. God knows what harm may come of it," she said.

"I will go alone," cried Cynthia, determinedly; "and then perhaps harm *will* come of it," and she snatched the seal skin coat off nurse's arm.

Nurse rose from her knees, and without another word wrapped it round Cynthia's slender figure, and throwing a long water-proof cloak over all, she followed the young girl ; who stole lightly down the back-stairs and away into the park, where the stars, shining like diamonds overhead, were all the light they had to guide their footsteps. Cynthia walked firmly, and without the slightest hesitation, but nurse stumbled perpetually, and—though she said no word —her sighs at each false step were loud and frequent.

Miss Castle dosed on in the drawing-room until roused by the butler bringing in tea; but she was too sleepy to heed anything so dosed off again, more soundly than before, until she was disturbed by, and conscious of a hand being laid on her shoulder. She started with a half-smothered cry. It was Sir Cyrus. The urn hissed on the table; and Raymond Bedfield, who stood facing her with his back to the fire, had his small crafty eyes fixed on her searchingly and thoughtfully.

She was quite awake now.

" We are waiting tea," said Sir Cyrus ; " where is Cynthia ?"

"I am so sorry; so very sorry. I had not an idea it was so late."

"Where is Miss Bedfield?" asked the baronet, once more.

"Is she not here?" said she, looking round. "Ah! she does not know it is tea time. I will fetch her."

She went—was gone ten—twenty minutes; and then, with a scared look on her face, came back without her.

"Where is Miss Bedfield?" asked Sir Cyrus, once more, and this time more sternly.

"I—I do not know. I—I—"

The cup and saucer Sir Cyrus held, clattered on to the floor and lay shattered in a dozen fragments. He strode to where Miss Castle had tremblingly seated herself, and seized her arm.

"Where is she? Speak, madam!" said he, his face white with rage.

"Ah! *Mon Dieu!* You hurt me. But—but how can I help it? She has worn her seal skin coat; and—and I cannot find that *vilaine femme,* her nurse!"

Was Sir Cyrus guilty of an oath as he brushed rudely past her towards the door?

"What is it, sir? Can I help you?" cried his nephew, hastily following him.

"No. Stay where you are, I command—nay, entreat, if you will."

In another moment Sir Cyrus had left the room, in ten minutes the house.

CHAPTER XV.

BROUGHT TO BAY.

RAYMOND BEDFIELD had looked on the foregoing scene with unqualified amazement. Had his uncle suddenly lost his senses, or Miss Castle, usually so calm and collected, been guilty of some rash indiscreet action? And why had the fact of his cousin having put on her seal skin coat—than what was more natural, seeing it was a chilly evening?—roused such violent anger on Sir Cyrus' part? He could have laughed outright at the—to him—absurdity of the thing, had it not been for

Miss Castle, who sat just where the baronet had left her, her white face and trembling, agitated state, being more mystifying than his uncle's sudden outburst of rage. Mr. Bedfield stood warming his coat tails before the fire, exactly opposite Miss Castle, evidently making a study of her face.

Presently she roused herself; the colour came back once more, and although her hands still shook, they grew steadier every moment.

She rose and rang the bell.

" You can take away," she said to the butler, who answered it, " and bring the wine."

The man looked round the room anxiously.

" Sir Cyrus has ordered his horse, miss," he said.

" I know it," she replied.

" I never knew him ride out so late; since—my lady died."

" There is a reason for it."

" God grant it's a good one," muttered the old man, as he placed the wine on the table.

Mr. Bedfield said nothing.

As soon as the man had gone, Miss Castle poured out some wine. When she had drank it, she turned to Mr. Bedfield.

"Why do you look at me so rudely? It would have been more polite had you rang the bell, or helped me to the wine. I am sure I needed it."

"To tell the truth, I am utterly bewildered. What in the name of heaven is all this row about?"

"Simply nothing."

"Oh! Ah! A likely story, and one I am not to be humbugged with."

"I am the most unlikely person in the world to humbug you."

"*You are,*" he replied, decidedly; "my uncle has not seen so much of human nature as I have."

"And therefore more easily humbugged you would say."

"And therefore more easily humbugged," he repeated.

Her eyes flamed, but she muttered softly,

" *Toujours gai, toujours souriante.*"

" That seems a favourite saying of yours," said Mr. Bedfield.

She did not answer; perhaps the sounds without prevented her, for just then a horse's hoofs rang out over the gravel beneath the terrace, then died away in the distance.

" That's my hot headed uncle. Don't you wish you could ride; but I do not think it is one of your many accomplishments. ' Over the hills and far away,' " said he, and then whistled the air as he stirred the fire.

Miss Castle rose steadily and stood before him, with her hands crossed meekly at her waist.

" Mr. Bedfield, you are rude, very rude to me —always rude to me now. What have I done to make you so? How have I incurred your ill will? I have no home, no friends, no money ; I am alone in the world and unprotected. Is it fair? is it right you should try and deprive me of all these? Is it manly of you? If you know

M 2

anything against me, or if you *think* you do, why
not accuse me at once ? I am not afraid. But
it is not right—it is not just, to hunt me down
because I have no one to stand up for me;" she
said all this quietly and softly, without the
slightest excitement or anger in her voice, but he
noticed that she never once raised her eyes to his.

What had he to accuse her of ? Simply nothing ;
only suspicions in which as yet there was no
certainty. She saw her advantage and pursued it.

" What do you accuse me of?" she asked.

" Nothing," he replied, hesitatingly.

" Then it is not brave, it is not generous of you
to try and take away my friends, to hunt me
down as you would a poor timid hare. Have you
no compassion in your big heart"—there was a
touch of sarcasm in her tone as she said this —
" for a helpless woman who has only herself to
fight for her ?" She had brought him to bay, indeed. He stood before her now as the accused,
not the accuser.

" What have I ever done to harm *you*?"

" Harm me? How absurd!" and he tried to laugh it off. " My dear Miss Castle, we are playing at cross purposes; every one seems to jump at conclusions, my uncle included."

" Then you accuse me of nothing?"

" Nothing. Absolutely nothing. There's my hand on it."

" No," she said, drawing back, " You have wounded me deeply, and I think you should say you are sorry."

" I *am* sorry you should have miscontrued my thoughtless words, regretted as soon as spoken;" but he bit his lip, and did not offer her his hand again.

" Thank you," she said, quietly.

" And now will you enlighten me as to all this hubbub about my little cousin and her seal skin coat."

" As also the cause of my fright. Is it not so?"

" Well, yes; I can't deny it."

"Ah!" said she, "you know nothing as to
the care and responsibility Miss Bedfield is to
me. You see me smiling and apparently happy,
and never think of the anxieties I have. How
should you? Cynthia has a temper, I don't
mean to say that it is worse than many girls'
tempers, but it is a wilful one, and when
thwarted, obstinate and determined. She has
been ill, as you know, and Sir Cyrus is most
anxious she should take the greatest care of herself, but instead of which, she wants to go out in
defiance of Mr. Gibbs even; in all weathers, no
matter whether it be rain or shine. For this
reason I promised Sir Cyrus I would never let
her out of my sight, but you see how it has been,
she has evaded me to-night and gone; and how
could I help it? how am I to blame when she has
been so determined and artful? I have done my
duty, but Sir Cyrus will not think so; he will
visit me with his severest displeasure, and can
you not see," said she, clasping her hands, and
this time really raising her eyes to his, "that if

anything happens to her—if she is really gone, I
shall be once more thrown on the world, and
what will become of me? where shall I go? Is
not the thought of going out into the world alone
enough to agitate any timid woman?"

Timid? Miss Castle timid, after the determined way in which she had set him down, but
now? And then her commanding figure, giving
the idea of power, those thin set lips, and strong
fingers, what signs of timidity were these? Was
she not rather a woman of nerve, who would
do battle in the world either with or against it.
Was it really the fear of being friendless that had
agitated her, or was it that she feared her golden
vision was fading away before she had grasped
it, or her airy visions crumbling beneath the breath
of Sir Cyrus' displeasure?

Raymond could not decide ; so he went out
on the terrace and smoked a cigar.

And now we must follow Sir Cyrus in his hasty
almost headlong ride to the station.

The train was about starting as he dismounted

from his horse and impetuously pushed past the late comers.

It was a short London train, and Sir Cyrus had no difficulty in looking into the several carriages as he went down the platform. But Cynthia was not there; and with a deep breath of relief he turned away, and then stood and watched until the whistle sounded, and the train flashed away out of his sight.

" When does the next train leave?" asked he, of the ticket collector.

" Where for, sir ?"

" Anywhere."

The man stared. " None due for the next two hours, sir."

" And after that ?"

" None before the night train."

Sir Cyrus turned on his heel, mounted his horse, and galloped homewards.

The sounds of his hasty return had scarcely ceased, ere Miss Castle found herself summoned to his presence. She went fully prepared for the

torrent of words she felt sure would be hurled at
her, and which she had been nerving herself for ever
since Mr. Bedfield had been smoking, and during
the time Sir Cyrus had had no thoughts but exciting, furious ones; even yet his temper was
still running wild within him, ready to boil over
at the slightest touch. He could not sit quietly
by the study fire devoured with vengeful, har-
rassing thoughts; so he sent for Miss Castle,
who, as calm and collected as he was fiery and
indignant, had him almost from the first at an
advantage.

Sir Cyrus looked up angrily as she entered, expecting to see a bold, daring look on her face; but
it was not so. She appeared meeker, more
humble than ever, with a beseeching, frightened
look in her dark grey eyes, which were filled with
tears, and so imploring looking in their expression, that the first angry words on Sir Cyrus'
tongue died away unuttered—almost forgotten;
but as yet he was not turned from his purpose

She must go—leave Stonycleft; that he was determined upon.

How little he knew of the powers of persuasion of a woman so clever as the chaperon!

" How comes this fatal neglect, madam; this unfaithful discharge of your duties as my daughter's chaperon? How account for 'the breaking of your promise to me? I hold a promise as sacred and binding, let the circumstances be what they will that tempt to break it. Had you expressed a fear as to your skill in fulfilling the compact, I would have imposed the task of—of restraining my daughter's will to another; as it is, you have betrayed the trust reposed in you— showed yourself unfitted for the task I had assigned you, of—of curbing my daughter's rebellious spirit, and therefore I must request you will resign your office here at once and for ever !"

Miss Castle never moved a muscle of her face; she still looked at him imploringly, and never attempted to stay his words—perhaps she thought it best he should give vent to a part of the violent feelings burning within him; but when he had ended, she burst into tears, and for once genuine ones. But Sir Cyrus was not apparently moved by them; he coughed nervously once or twice, and turned away his chair towards the fire, signifying as plainly as could be, that he desired the conference should end.

Then Miss Castle spoke.

" I will not attempt," said she, between her sobs, either real or assumed, " to refute any thing you say. I ought never to have lost sight of my charge for a single moment during the *day*, and I did not; I kept my promise faithfully—I did indeed, without a question as to why you imposed it on me; but you are not just when I say you have been unfaithful in my duties to Miss Bedfield, by allowing her to slip out after dark. That I have not done, seeing you never told me my surveillance was to be continued *then;* had you done so, I should never have lost sight of her, and forgive me, you would not have to deplore her— her absence now."

Sir Cyrus could not deny the justice of this. Miss Castle saw her advantage and kept it.

"If you have no other fault to find with me than this, you will not be so unjust as to send me away for what might have been avoided, had you but trusted me. Oh! Sir Cyrus, can you not see that—that I would obey you implicitly in any thing, no matter what; only try me—only trust me," said she, earnestly.

Could he trust her? He looked round at her searchingly.

"Oh, Sir Cyrus! you can trust me," exclaimed she, answering his look. "I would sooner lose my tongue than repeat any thing you tell me. You have been very, very kind to me since I have been at Stonycleft—no brother could have been kinder, and, with no one in the wide world who cares for me, I have felt your kindness grate-fully. Don't send me away! Pray don't! It will—will break my heart!" and her sobs burst forth again.

Perhaps Sir Cyrus was surprised at her words,

or the impassioned tone in which they were said, for he looked at her steadily, and his eyes were more searching — almost wondering in their expression. As Miss Castle saw them, her face became crimson, and she sobbed again as she covered it with her hands.

Sir Cyrus never removed his gaze.

He had calmed greatly when next he spoke.

"Perhaps," said he, "I have been too hasty, I am apt to be so."

"No, no. Not too hasty. Never too hasty with me;" and she took her hands away from her face, so that Sir Cyrus could see it quite plainly now; see also its agitation, without the help of her trembling, shaking form.

"Sit down," he said, kindly, reaching her a chair.

She sat down, and, laying her face on her hands, began sobbing bitterly.

"Hush!" he said; "there is nothing to be afraid of. Why should you fear me?" and he bent over her as she sat, looking anything but like the stern, angry Sir Cyrus of a few minutes since.

Did he take her hand and draw it towards him? Miss Castle scarcely knew, for a soft voice said ;

" Papa, I am here.   Do you want me?"

Cynthia had opened the door without either being aware of it, and now stood close behind the chaperon's chair.

CHAPTER XVI.

AS CRAFTY AS A FOX.

WITH a look of surprise and anger on her face,
Cynthia stood before her father's startled gaze in
her seal-skin coat and hat; she had evidently but
just returned home.

She could not have made her appearance at a
more inopportune moment; one short hour earlier
and Sir Cyrus would have given the half he
possessed to know that she was safe, and not, as
he feared, lured into a disgraceful flight with
Frederick Alywin; but now for the haughty, im-

penetrable baronet to be caught— if not making
love, at least very nearly akin to it, and that with
no high born dame, but the lowly dependent—the
chaperon and *ci-devant* governess! What wonder
that Sir Cyrus was confused, and not a little
ashamed of himself! while Miss Castle was even
more abashed than he ; nevertheless, she was the
first to recover—to stand up and face the intruder
albeit her cheeks were flushed, and her eyes heavy
with recent tears.

"*Dieu soit benit*," said, fervently ; " we
feared, I know not what."

"You feared I had not gone," returned
Cynthia, scornfully. "My father that I had—
was it not so?" and she turned at once to Sir
Cyrus, and asked, " Why did you fear?—was it
because you thought you had by your harsh
conduct driven me to disgrace the name of Bedfield? If so, you need have had no fear; for as
long as *you* hold the honour of our ancient house
untarnished," and she shot a quick, passionate
glance at Miss Castle, " so long will I."

Her words incensed Sir Cyrus; his anger had not wholly died out; it had been slumbering for awhile like a lull in a violent storm.

" Where have you been ?" he thundered.

" I have been out in the park," she answered, without hesitation.

" At this hour!—close upon ten o'clock? You do well, girl, to talk and boast so boldly of the honour of our ancient house, when every serving man—if he knew of it—would wag his finger at you for this shameless moonlight stroll."

Her eyes flashed as angrily as his.

" You dare not," she said, "even in thought, accuse me of anything wrong. You know better. Besides, nurse was with me."

" Where ?" he cried, fiercely.

" Down by the coppice."

" To meet?—speak out! to meet—?"

She went over, with pale face and compressed lips, to where Sir Cyrus stood.

" I will whisper it," she said.

" Speak out! There is no need of secrecy.

You have broken down that barrier by your conduct to-night."

She drew back a step; hesitated; and then said, bravely and firmly,

" Frederick Alywin !"

Sir Cyrus showed no surprise, but he glanced at Miss Castle, whose face expressed the utmost dismay and astonishment.

" You have dared !" said he, vehemently.

" I have dared," she said.

" Girl! don't beard me—don't defy me too much—don't work me into a fury that men, strong men, have before now trembled at."

" Oh, papa," she said, " he goes away in two days' time, and I shall not see him again for months—perhaps years—if ever. I could not let him go without a word—I should have died first."

" I will take care he goes for ever," he said, angrily.

" You will not harm him," she said, all her anger and courage vanishing in a moment when her fears were roused, "you will not harm him, whose only fault is loving me so dearly?"

"Harm him?—he is not worth harming. A low-born serf! But let him come once more within the reach of my arm, and he shall feel it again for this fresh insult that he has flung in my face. As for you, since you are so anxious to be mated, I will find you a husband before many hours are over; one who, if I mistake not, will curb your proud spirit, break your rebellious will as though it were a sapling."

"You dare not—shall not force me against my will," she said.

"Come away," whispered her chaperon, with pale lips, "come away."

And Cynthia suffered herself to be led away up to her room, where nurse awaited her in fear and trepidation.

"Fear nothing," said Miss Castle; "Sir Cyrus is angry and enraged at your thwarting his will. He will think and say differently to-morrow."

" How can you tell?" cried Cynthia. " You who, like a snake in the grass, have poisoned his mind with your envenomed tongue, been leading him like a lamb to the slaughter, with your insidious, artful smiles, and fawning ways. Ah! no doubt you gloried in my absence, and had I not returned when I did, might have reigned here as mistress before another week."

" I—I ?" cried Miss Castle, in well-feigned astonishment.

" Yes, you. Ah! you think I have not seen it—you think you have been too deep and wary for me? I laugh—child as you think me—at such thin skinned schemes. Go! I defy you to win over my father. When you think him caught in your trap, then look to yourself!"

" What do you mean?" cried Miss Castle.

" That you are an impostor, whom some day I hope to unmask."

" You shall do that now," said she, sitting down quietly.

" Just hear her, nurse," said Cynthia, rudely;

" did you ever know one of our house frightened into a concession?"

" Never! God help me!" said nurse.

" You hear?" continued Cynthia, looking at Miss Castle.

" I do. But they may never have had one so determined to deal with. I have a right to know what you hint at so darkly."

" I acknowledge no right—none; neither now, nor hereafter, let what will happen."

" She'll be ill with all this talk," cried nurse; " a delicate blossom like this to have such a heap of worry. If her poor lady mother had only lived to see it."

" She would never have lived and seen either that, or the face of the lady who sits opposite," returned Cynthia.

" Hush! hush! my darling! Will you please leave her, miss?"

" Not until she tells me what she has heard against me."

" Heard !—what should she have heard? She's only striving to hear," said nurse, incautiously.

" Striving to hear?" said Miss Castle, with a laugh. "' Ah! I am glad of that, as I hope what she hears of poor me, will disabuse her mind of the strange prejudice she has conceived against me. Then, I hope she will give me credit for doing better things than these dreadful sins she accuses me of," and she went out and shut the door.

" I defy her !" thought she, as she wended her way down-stairs; "defy both her and *him!* What can she, poor little fly, do? and, as for *him*, I am as strong and brave as he."

As she reached the hall, she almost fell over Nero, who lay stretched at full length on the mat.

Miss Castle trembled and shuddered as she thought of the beating Raymond Bedfield had once given him.

" He is a terrible enemy to have," she muttered, as she opened the drawing-room door, where sat, not Sir Cyrus, of whom she probably came in quest, but *her enemy*, as she was pleased to style him.

" I thought you had gone to bed," she said.

" Did you? I believe half-past ten is the orthodox hour here; but I am sitting, not idling my time away as at a cursory glance you might be led to suppose, but thinking—thinking deeply."

" Is that anything so very unusual?" asked she.

"Well, I rather think it is, or was before I visited Stonycleft.

" Did you never sit thinking, then?"

" Very seldom—if ever."

" And what has changed you so suddenly?"

" Many things suspicious and unsuspicious."

" Ah! now you deal in enigmas, which my poor little brain," and she pressed her hand to her forehead, " is too dull and stupid to solve."

" There is no solving my enigma; it is a mystery."

" Always a mystery ?"

" No, not always. I shall, perhaps, fathom it."

" And when you do ?"

" Then it shall no longer be a mystery."

" As how so ?"

" I shall scatter it to the winds far and wide."

" And near," she said.

" Just so," he replied.

" You would be a dangerous man to make an enemy of, determined, fearless, pitiless," and she thought of Nero. " Alas ! for the woman whose character you might hold in your hands, to make or mar at your pleasure."

" You are wrong. My heart can feel compassion for even a fallen angel, but she must be a repentant one, no plotter or schemer, no destroyer of a family's peace. Then ——" he hesitated and stopped suddenly.

" Then ?" inquired Miss Castle.

" Then I would be pitiless. Hunt her down without mercy or compassion."

"And would succeed if it were possible. You are crafty as well as unmerciful."

"Crafty? Well, I have thought lately I could be even that. I should not belie the look in my eyes if I were."

"Or the look in your eyes when you first came to Stonycleft," she said, boldly, "but that look has almost left them now; circumstances over which the heart has no control, alter cases wonderfully."

She had certainly silenced him, for he made no reply. She looked as though half expecting one, and then seeing he did not speak, she said:

"Will you tell me what you are thinking of?"

"Thinking, as the lad said, of what I ought to be thinking of?" replied he, laughing.

"That was of Cynthia, then."

"Of Cynthia, Sir Cyrus, and lastly of yourself."

"Still of me," she said, "that is hardly fair."

"Why not?"

"I thought we had settled all that at tea-time."

"And so we did," he replied, looking her steadily in the face, " but thoughts are not under the control of one's will, and old familiar faces are apt to come back unasked, and sometimes unwelcome."

The very faintest tint of colour flushed her face ; but it was no time for flinching, no time for timidity. She returned his gaze, but to his surprise, her eyes were sorrowful, and he almost thought, suffused with tears.

This ; so different to the angry look he had ex-pected, staggered him. He ceased his scrutiny at once, and looked uncomfortably away at the dying embers of the fire.

"You have treated me very *cavalierly* to-night," she said ; "why have you done so?"

"Pray do not let us begin the old story over again," he said.

"You have taken a dislike to me. Is it not so?" she asked, unheeding his remark.

"No," he answered, " No——" but he hesitated.

" I see it is so," she said.

" Why should I not turn the tables and ask
why you dislike me ?" said he, trying to laugh it
off.

"I am but a poor chaperon, a nobody, far
below the heir of Stonycleft, whose lands and
possessions extend for miles round, and in whose
veins flows the blood of the proud Percys. How
could I even in thought dare dislike you ?"

Her tone was one of utter humility, than which
none knew better than the chaperon how to
assume.

" You are too clever for me, Miss Castle," said
Mr. Bedfield, rising; " It will take all my
craft," and he laughed, "my wisdom and skill,
to be a match for you."

" You will never cease to suspect and persecute
me," she said, in a mournful tone; "But, *chacun
porte sa croix*, and I have mine and must bear
it."

" It is very cold, the fire is all but out," he said.

" Are you going? Good-night, Mr. Bedfield," and she held out her hand.

" Nay, fair lady. I will not treat you so *cavalierly* as to leave you to the tender mercies of the ghosts of my ancestors, who, according to tradition, were a bloodthirsty race. Who knows but that the Percy—so famed for his ill deeds and wicked murder of the fair Alice, his wife—might not take it into his head to walk to-night in search of something more exciting still."

" And what then? I am not afraid," she said.

" But others are for you," he replied, as he held open the door for her to pass out.

Was it done with a purpose to prevent her meeting with Sir Cyrus again that night? Miss Castle thought so, as she bit her lips with vexation, and went away up stairs to her room.

Mr. Bedfield watched her until the light from the candle she carried vanished from his sight.

" A woman," muttered he, as he prepared to

follow her, "who would talk a man into destroying his own soul for her. A very tigress in revenge; a very fox in cunning; and a handsome, a very handsome woman. Pshaw! I shall be falling in love with her myself if I don't take care. As it is, I am scarcely her match even in a war of words."

CHAPTER XVII.

CHECKMATE INTERRUPTED.

Miss Castle reached her room in anger and vexation at Mr. Bedfield's having baffled her in her wish of seeing Sir Cyrus; there was also an undefined fear of him lurking in her heart, which she vainly tried to shake off.

" It will be a fierce, deadly battle; a strife that must slay one of us. No temporising; no bloodless struggle; no half measures, but a mortal combat and a ruthless conqueror, that will *he* be.

How I hate him !" said she, as she placed the light on the toilet table.

But all angry feelings fled, and were superseded by rapturous ones, as she saw the small note lying within reach of her hand. It was from Sir Cyrus ; a glance told her that, and with a cry of exultation, she snatched it, and pressed it to her bosom.

She stood thus for a moment, then raised the small missive high in the air, and fluttered it round her head, as though she, having led a forlorn hope, and reached the goal unhurt and in safety ; had seized the banner, waved it aloft, and cried Victory !

She calmed her excitement presently, and sat down, with her pulses beating as quickly, if not quicker, than when she fancied she felt Sir Cyrus' hand on hers. But the note was different to what she had been expecting. It was no love epistle, penned hastily and warmly before the writer had had time to cool. There was not a word in it that could be construed into a tender one.

It was no victory yet. She had exulted too soon. Sir Cyrus was not a man to compromise himself in writing; every word had been weighed, and written carefully and cautiously.

"Thursday night.

"DEAR MADAM,

"May I ask you to kindly resume your duties as chaperon to my daughter, as after due thought, I agree with you in thinking that she still needs some little control and management. Her will is unfortunately an obstinate one, and her temper requires correcting. The name we unfortunately heard will, I am sure, be held sacred by both you and me. It is a folly that will die out of itself.

"Yours faithfully,

"CYRUS BEDFIELD."

"Not if I can help it," cried Miss Castle, as she carefully reclosed the letter.

How she wished she had not quarelled with

Mrs. Alywin! An idle wish, as she felt, but one she could not help her thoughts dwelling on. Could she but get speech of the son, before he went to India, so as to worm out on what kind of footing he and Cynthia stood to each other? Another idle wish, as he would be gone in two days, and how could she manage a meeting so soon, so hastily as that?

Miss Castle answered Sir Cyrus' note before going to bed. She simply stated her willingness to continue on as Cynthia's chaperon, and hoped she should manage better in that capacity than she had hitherto done, by striving with care and kindness to check his daughter's temper and will. His wishes on the subject should be her constant study, and she hoped in time he would see a material change for the better.

"There," said she, as she finished it, "I have a great mind to show it to Cynthia, and then give it to my 'enemy' to deliver to his uncle; he would be sure to read it; at least, I should if I were he."

Before putting away Sir Cyrus' letter, she read it over again, dwelling on each word ; but all to no purpose, no double meaning could she detect, turn and twist the sentences as she would ; and she was forced unwillingly to confess that the new-born hopes she had indulged in on first seeing it on the table, were premature.

She took out two letters from her desk, with which she placed the one she held in her hand, and tied them round with a piece of string. It did not fit very closely when she had knotted it.

" So much the better. I shall be sure to have some more some day," said she, as she closed and locked her desk, and then bethought her of how she should meet Sir Cyrus, and how she should behave when she saw him alone on the morrow.

But neither the next day, nor for many days after, did Miss Castle succeed in obtaining a tête-à-tête with Sir Cyrus. She never had the opportunity. Either purposely or by accident it was never allowed her. In the morning it was

Cynthia ; in the afternoon Mr. Bedfield ; in the evening both. She was never alone with him. Did the cousins work together, or did each strive for one and the same end, without the other being aware of it ? Miss Castle could not decide, and with all her cunning, was at fault. She never detected a glance in either that spoke of mutual understanding, never came accidentally upon them talking mysteriously together, so that they broke off suddenly when they saw her. If they did form plans together, it was in a way and by a means she knew not, and which baffled her.

Sir Cyrus never reverted to the scene in the study, either by word or token. He met her as calmly polite, as rigidly courteous as ever. He gave her no warmer pressure of the hand as she wished him good-night, no look that could be construed into a tender one, and yet Miss Castle's mind and will were as active and determined as ever. If Cynthia had but fled with Frederick Alywin ?—*if* she and Sir Cyrus had not been interrupted ?—*if* she could only get him to talk to her alone? Miss Castle's thoughts were mostly *ifs* now; possibilities that might have been—that might be, and yet were not. *If*—but that was the mightiest *if* of all— *if* Sir Cyrus could only be brought to propose to his nephew—as he had threatened—a marriage between himself and cousin?—*if* such a thing could be brought about?—then the chaperon's cause was won.

Miss Castle judged that Mr. Bedfield was not a man to have a marriage thrust upon him, whether he willed it or no. He was one who would woo a woman; win her by the strength of his love, not by the force of his will. He would not marry his cousin as she stood with him now, nay, more Miss Castle felt he did not desire it; but was rather striving against any tender feeling that might, by any possibility, arise in his heart ·for her. How almost coldly he had borne himself towards her since that night on which he had met her out so late in the park, when he had been smoking. Had he not questioned and cross-questioned the chaperon about it, but to no purpose; she was even there too deep for him, and gloried in it. It was a kind of first defeat, and she heralded it as an omen of good.

It was long since Sir Cyrus and the chaperon had played backgammon together. Was the baronet wary of her smiles, or did he fear to trust himself under the shadow of her grey eyes, lest they should obtain an influence over him impossible to shake off?—or did he fear any presumption on her part from the foolish act into which his compassionate feelings had so basely betrayed him? Whatever the cause, it was days before he proposed as of old to sit down and play; and then, how cautious Miss Castle was!—how careful not to alarm him, by a word or look that might put him on his mettle, or be construed by him into a covert desire of obtaining an undue ascendency over his weak heart. Without doubt, she *was* as cunning as a fox, and played her cards well.

What possibility was there of exciting conver-

sations in which she had a way of leading words,
and sentences to work her own will ; or of soft
honied speeches wherewith to lure the victim on;
since Cynthia never went near the piano now,
never played a note, but sat and chatted with
her cousin close by, or played at chess at a table
drawn near the fire, by which—the evenings
being set in for cold—her father and the chaperon
sat ; but Cynthia was foolish indeed, if she
thought her close proximity would prevent or
deter the other's schemes ; she worked too well,
was working too well.

One evening, the fourth on which the backgammon had been resumed, it was Sir Cyrus' turn
to throw ; but there was no sound of the dice rattling; Sir Cyrus' thoughts were not with the
game; his eyes were not on the board, but on
Miss Castle's face.

" It is your turn, Sir Cyrus," she said, in her
softest tones.

He threw; but at random. Played ; but played
badly, and gathered up the dice again absently.

Then Miss Castle played, and then—not Sir
Cyrus, no; she had to wait again.

Sir Cyrus was certainly absent.   The dice-box
lay unheeded on the table beside him.

Miss Castle looked towards the chess players.
Mr. Bedfield had just given 'check,' and both he
and Cynthia seemed apparently intent on their
game.

Lightly the chaperon laid her fingers on the
baronet's.

" It is your turn to play," she said.

" A thousand pardons," he exclaimed, rousing
up.

" You are tired; is it not so ?"

" With such an adversary it is impossible," he
replied, softly, but his thoughts seemed still to
be wandering.   And his eyes—ah ! what did
she read in his eyes to cause her face to flush
crimson, as she looked at him half-respectfully,
half-consciously, as she met his earnest gaze.

However scheming, however sinful—if sinful
she was—the chaperon might be, she had not

lost the great charm of beauty in woman; she still blushed as easily as a child, or rather Sir Cyrus had the power of making her do so.

Had they but been alone! so she sighed, as she met Sir Cyrus' almost impassioned gaze Alone! The chess-table clattered down, falling the chessmen against the fender,· on to the carpet, and in all directions.

"Ah! goodness!" cried Miss Castle, as she hastily rose.

" Did you cry *mon Dieu?*" asked Mr. Bedfield as he stooped to pick up the unlucky chess-men.

" I did not; such a cry would shock your English ears."

" Or murder! like one of Duncan's guards?"

" Nor that, neither," she replied, steadily.

" Who did the mischief?" asked Sir Cyrus.

" I," said Cynthia, laughing.   " It was very wrong of me, but I could not bear the thoughts of being beaten; so I stopped a checkmate, as I always shall;" and she looked defiantly at Miss Castle.

"Chess," said Sir Cyrus, "is not a game to suit a Bedfield; it tries the temper too much. Why not give us some music? Charm us with your siren voice?"

"I have hurt my finger, papa. If I do sing, Miss Castle must please play the accompaniment."

How Miss Castle wished she had sprained her wrist. She went to the piano, and as she sat waiting for the music Cynthia was searching for, she unconsciously removed her bracelet, and pressed her fingers tightly over her wrist; then moved it about as though to try the soundness of the muscle.

"It is not sprained," said Mr. Bedfield, guessing her thoughts. "Do you wish it was?"

She looked at him almost fiercely   But there was no trace of anger in her voice, as she replied,

"My bracelet is so tight, it always hurts my wrist."

I have said that Mr. Bedfield generally inter-

cepted Miss Castle's plans or designs of an afternoon; Cynthia of a morning.　Where then did
the latter spend her afternoons?　Ah! this question had puzzled the chaperon, and one day she
watched her, dogged her footsteps, and discovered
her seated on the sill of one of the windows in
the picture gallery, with a book in her lap; her
face, not leaning over its pages, but almost flat-
tened against the glass, as she rested her forehead
on its framework.　She did not perceive Miss
Castle, so intent was she, either in thought, or in
gazing earnestly at something beyond.

"You here, Cynthia!" said she, to the startled
girl.　"Is there anything to be seen?" and
pressing her face also close to the glass, she
looked below—beyond—everywhere.

"Nothing but the park," replied Cynthia,
"which at this time of the year looks dull
enough."

"What a strange place for you to have chosen
for reading in.　All these lords and high-born
dames in their satins and velvets, their frills and

farthingales, Spanish hats and feathers, not to mention their diamonds, which I can almost fancy I see sparkle, so true has the painter been ; make me feel melancholy. It is so sad to think that the wearers are all dead and gone. I wonder whether they died old or young? However it was ; there is uo more happiness or misery, sin or sorrow, virtues or vices for them to answer for. That lady over there, with the small ruff round her fair throat, reminds me of Queen Elizabeth ; what a sad face, and yet how beautiful in its repose and sadness."

" Really, Miss Castle, you should write a history of the Bedfield family, gathered from looking at their portraits. That Queen Elizabeth—as you are pleased to style her—is the fair Lady Alice."

" Indeed ! She does not look sinful. So fair a face could surely not have hidden a false heart ?"

" I believe she was as good as she was beautiful. It was her husband 'The Percy,' who had the false heart. He was famed for every crime under the sun ; or, I suppose, I should apostrophise the moon, as men did not, I conclude, even in his day, run away with fair maidens, or commit murder—certainly not the latter—in the light of broad day."

" Ah ! *pauvre dâme*, she deserves the prayer her sad, sweet looks seem to ask. And which is her husband ? And why is he called ' The Percy ?' "

" Because he was the first of that name, and the only one, I believe, who deigned to ally himself by marriage with our house. A noble alliance they call it. Noble ! I shame to think any of his bad blood flows in my veins. He was a traitor—not to his country—that he served well and faithfully, but to his best friend, as also to his wife. He murdered her."

" Alas ! poor lady !"

" I hate the very sight of his picture," cried Cynthia ; " that is the one, whose wicked eyes are looking at me as I sit. He brought sin, sorrow, and shame—no one calls it dishonour—upon us. And yet they talk of the Lady Alice's noble marriage. Do you see his crafty look, his peaked beard, and wicked eyes? with his hand on the rapier at his side, ready to attack, or even stab his dearest friend? perhaps parry some murderous assault he feared, or lived in dread of; for, stained with crime, he must have had enemies. Then look at the other hand hidden away in his doublet, and holding—perhaps while the man painted his portrait—a more murderous weapon than the rapier, one ready to be flashed forth in an instant on an emergency. Do you see the dark look on his face? his coal black eyes and hair? I sit here and watch him often, and always with the same result—the same conclusion."

" And what is that?" asked Miss Castle.

" That you and he are wonderfully alike. You might be taken for brother and sister."

"If you mean in wickedness," replied Miss Castle, " then you have been neither compli-

mentary nor just, but if you mean in outward face
and form, then I thank you for the flattery, as I
see no wicked look in 'The Percy's ' eyes ; they
appear to me fiery indeed, but capable of a whole
world of love. Then what a noble brow! surely
no craft ever lurked there. His mouth is hidden
by the long silken moustache, but I am sure it is
well shaped and smiling,from the whole expression
of the countenance. True, he lays his hand on
his rapier, but it is so lightly the fingers cannot
be said to grasp it, while the hand itself looks as
soft and shapely as a woman's, and as unlike one
stained with murder as possible. Then the hand
hidden away in his doublet, may be to grasp
nothing more deadly than a true love knot."

"I am glad you draw so flattering a portrait.
To me ' The Percy,' can never look other than
wicked and crafty. But you can turn and twist
everything as you will it ; even a bad man's
portrait. There are some verses about him that
nurse knows by heart. They give you the whole
terrible account of how he murdered his wife and

buried her at the foot of the turret stairs, and
how she sat there ever afterwards at the same
hour—the dead of night—and would sit until the
deed was avenged."

" And was it ever avenged ?"

" I am sure I do not know, and don't much
care. I have never seen the ghost, and don't
know any one who has, not even old Nursey,"
laughed she, "and I know she believes in it
firmly."

" But what is this bit of paper, stuck in the
picture frame ?"

" That ! " cried Cynthia, starting up. " That
is mine. I must have left it there the other
day."

" It is mine now, or rather your father's. I
shall take it to him."

" Oh, take it by all means ; and much good
may it do you," replied Cynthia, hastily, for she
had caught sight of Nurse from the window as
she stood up, and her whole frame trembled
with excitement, while her face glowed and

flushed with pleasure, and she let Miss Castle go away without another word of remonstrance.

She stood listening until the latter's footsteps died away, then she fled swiftly to her room, and when nurse entered it,—which she did a moment after,—flung her arms round the old woman's neck.

" Lord-a-mercy ! don't throttle me."

" Give me the letter then ! Dear old Nursey, give it quick."

" Ah, the impatience of young hearts! If I'd known she'd have hugged my poor old bones so, I'd never have given her the signal, of putting up the veil off my face. I'd have worn two and never lifted either of 'em till she'd the letter safe in her hand or at her lips, as 'tis now. Ah ! well-a-day ! I mind when I was just as foolish, but it's best to be more sober at it ; men don't like them mad fits."

The paper Miss Castle had so coolly walked off with, she read as she [passed through one of the corridors, and again as she halted for a moment in front of the large stained glass window on the stairs.

"When a woman as crafty as 'The Percy' shall plot.
Let the heir then beware, lest an heir he is not.
But the woman shall fall."   *   *   *   *

The rest was carefully effaced, and hold the paper up to the light, or which way she would, Miss Castle could not decipher the words; but her face glowed with something more than pleasure as she refolded the paper carefully and placed it in her bosom, and then snapped her fingers as derisively as she had done, on the day on which she had parted from Mrs. Alywin so wrathfully by the plantation.

" They please me, these lines," she said, " they please me much. While as for the threatening words of the last! I laugh at and dare them!" and she went on with a half triumphant step towards the " Blue room."

CHAPTER XVIII.

REFUSING TO BE CAST ADRIFT.

THE "Blue Room," so called from the colour of its furniture, was smaller than many of those habitually tenanted at Stonycleft; perhaps for this reason it had been chosen by Cynthia to sit in of an afternoon. Besides the fact of its being warm and pleasant, it looked out on to the flower garden, which in summer time was a mass of many coloured flowers, filling the air around both far and near with their sweet scents; now of course it was void of flowers, but the shining green leaves of the laurels and small white blossoms of the laurestine were grateful to the eye amidst the dull wintry-growing aspect without. The room was not unoccupied when Miss Castle entered it; Mr. Bedfield was standing at the window, guilty of the very bad habit of uttering his thoughts aloud.

" My Heaven !" he said, " thrown at me like a ball of worsted !"

Miss Castle heard the words distinctly, saw the indignant, angry expression of his face as he turned it towards her, and her heart gave a great bound as she guessed what had irritated him.

He had been closeted with Sir Cyrus since lunch, and when tired of being alone she had gone in search of, and dogged Cynthia's footsteps. Had Sir Cyrus mooted. the question of a marriage between his daughter and nephew? Had the latter declined the honour of the alliance ? And had they quarrelled ? All this crossed her mind in a moment.

Miss Castle was partly right. The Baronet

had hinted at such a marriage; but although the
nephew had met his uncle's advances coldly,
they had not quarrelled, indignant as the former
had been—not for himself, but for his cousin.
In thought, he accused his uncle of greed; greed
for his daughter, even to the bartering her; for
it was a barter, a mercenary bargain, seeing that
Sir Cyrus allowed there was little or no love between the cousins; that was to come. To come!
and she, although so young, with a heart as strong
to love and suffer,—if need be,—for that love,
as any woman's. Then the insult to himself. A
wife thrown into his arms, whether he willed it
or no; a wife who, the giver allowed, did not as
yet love him, but the chances were that she
might. What wonder, Raymond Bedfield re-
jected such a proposition with a touch of scorn
and bitterness! They had it is true parted
apparently good friends, yet the nephew was
venting his suppressed rage by uttering his
thoughts aloud, and alone—as he thought—in the
" Blue Room," while as for the uncle; would he

take such a refusal quietly, or would his hot passionate blood resent it?

Miss Castle said not a word to Mr. Bedfield, but drew near the table and took up some unfinished work that she had left there that morning. She had scarcely taken the needle in her hand, when one of the footmen entered with the afternoon's letters, on a small silver salver. He drew near Miss Castle and held it towards her.

There were two letters. As she looked at them the bright triumphant look faded away and her face assumed in a moment an almost ghastly appearance. She clutched hold of one of the letters as though her fingers were a vice, while at the same moment she flashed a look at the man at her side. But he was dull or purposely misunderstood her. "That is Mr. Bedfield's, miss," he said. She dropped it. It was a thin letter, and the envelope bore a foreign stamp.

" A letter for me!" cried Mr. Bedfield, coming forward.

It was handed him. He took it up, all

crushed as it was by the tight pressure of Miss
Castle's fingers, and walked away with it in his
hand towards the fire ; before which he stood—
as men selfishly do, whether alone or in a room
full of company,—warming his coat tails, and
reading the address.

"From Fred Stanhope! I should know his
scrawly hand among a thousand; no one but
himself ever wrote such a fist. How well I
remember those few days we passed together
in Rome, three years ago! So ·he has gone
back there again, has he?" said he, examining
the postage stamp.

Then there was a crumpling and crackling
of paper as Mr. Bedfield opened it, and then—
then it was snatched from his grasp and on
the blazing fire in the grate.

"Ah!" exclaimed he, irefully ; " why did you
do that?" and he rudely pushed Miss Castle aside
as he made a snatch at the burning letter. But
he was too late. It was in a blaze ; the thinness
of the paper hastening its untimely fate.

He turned in a tempest of rage to the chaperon.

"Why did you do that? How dare you do that?"

She stood close by his side, the same ghastly look on her face, one hand pressed tightly over her heart as though to still its wild beating.

Their eyes met.

It was but a momentary glance, but in that glance Mr. Bedfield discovered her.

"My God!" he cried, staggering back.

The letter was a heap of ashes now; and with that danger, whatever it was, past, Miss Castle was growing calm, and the guilty, terrified look disappearing. Only her lips seemed rigid, as she asked, half ironically,

"Are you ill? Shall I call any one?"

"Ill? Call any one? Ain't you afraid to?"

"No. I never felt braver in my life."

"And yet I tell you, I know you; have discovered you, and the whole villany you would be guilty of."

"You are mistaken."

"Not so by Heaven! The scales have fallen from my eyes. I will unmask you to Sir Cyrus, and that at once," said he, impetuously.

"Very well. I shall demand proof of whatever falsehood you assert."

Proof? She spoke cunningly and at advantage, as she always did. What proof had he?— None. The letter might have contained it, but that was gone; that and his friend's address.

"Woman! have you no shame?" he said.

"None. Seeing I have nothing to be ashamed of. Where are your proofs?" she said, half ironically. "Do you not shame to speak as you are doing to a defenceless woman; and one, too, under the protection of your uncle's roof?"

"Hold! we will not wage words which answer no purpose whatever. I will bring proofs of what I—I know to be true. I will do more, I will fetch them."

He rang the bell. "Carter," said he, to the man who answered it. "It's ten to four; when does the next train leave for London?"

" Half-past, sir."

" Good. Desire Jackson to have my portman-teau ready, and the trap at the door to start to meet that train.''

Mr. Bedfield drew a long breath and sat down to think, not so very far from Miss Castle, who plied her needle apparently unconcerned, but his every action and word filling her heart with dread and fear.

" You are a bitter, revengeful enemy to have," she said, " you jump at some insane conclusion, and then hunt me down for it."

" Not so. I will be a generous enemy," for his anger had somewhat cooled, " I will not hunt you down without mercy. I swear that if you will leave this house at once and for ever, I will give up my journey to Rome; nay more, will never say a word of—of what I know as long as I live."

" And this you call mercy? Sending me forth on a bare suspicion to get my bread as best I can! Truly I thank you for it, and would make you my best curtsey if I were standing."

"Very well," said he, biting his lip, "then war let it be. I go to excuse myself to Sir Cyrus, and my cousin, and then for my journey."

But Sir Cyrus was in the room as he spoke.

"Going! going away? This is sharp work. I trust there is no offence, nephew?"

"Offence, sir! None at all. My sudden departure perhaps is not very courteous, but I have received some bad news by the post, which renders a journey to town indispensable."

"Mrs. Bedfield?" began the baronet.

"Is well. I am not going home as yet, indeed my absence will not extend over a week, when if you will allow me, I will return and conclude my visit here."

"I am sure I—we shall all be delighted," said the baronet, but he did not give the invitation very heartily.

There was a silence while Mr. Bedfield wrote a few hasty lines with his pencil in his pocket-book. He tore the leaf out and gave it to the chaperon.

" This address will always find me," said he meaningly, " should you—as I hope you will—change your mind."

" Jackson is at the door, waiting, sir," said Carter, throwing open the door.

With a hasty adieu to Sir Cyrus, Mr. Bedfield went out.

" One moment," said he, as he almost leapt up the stairs to where he saw his cousin standing.

She was coming down, but waited for him on the top stair.

" I'm off !" said he, excitedly, "not to Charles-town ; but to London, Paris, Rome, etc. If you write, address *Poste Restante*. Good-bye."

Cynthia was indeed astonished. " Going ?—going?" he said, doubtingly.

"Aye! To unmask the chaperon," he whispered. " I have a clue, a certain one. Keep up your spirits until I return. *She* will never be your stepmother."

" You will return, and soon ?" asked Cynthia, eagerly.

" Yes, in a week, if possible. But write if you are in trouble, or if anything should be amiss, and address always, *Poste restante.*"

He wrung her hand and was gone.

Cynthia stood half bewildered. Then, as if suddenly recollecting something, fled swiftly after him on to the terrace.

"*Poste restante* where ? Where ?" she screamed.

But the echo of her silvery voice could not reach her cousin. He was even then crashing round the corner of the drive.

" Lord ! How them Bedfields do drive," exclaimed the groom; " blest if he don't most beat the master at it."

Miss Castle sat in the " blue room," weeping passionate tears.

What man is proof against a woman's tears, especially a pretty woman's ? Sir Cyrus might be proud and haughty, but his heart was as soft and susceptible as other men's hearts.

"She will never be your stepmother!" said Mr. Bedfield to his cousin, yet the sound of the wheels bearing him so swiftly from Stonycleft, had scarcely died away in the distance, before the chaperon was his uncle's affianced wife.

CHAPTER XIX.

THE BITER BIT.

MR. Bedfield was of a sluggish nature, rarely guilty of a rash impetuous act, yet he travelled almost night and day.   On! Onward! scarcely allowing himself an hour's rest at his halting stations.   His thoughts harassed him, and precluded the idea of wholesome sound sleep. Would his friend Fred Stanhope be still in Rome? Should he succeed in obtaining the clue he sought ; the proof that the chaperon was other than she professed herself to be?   All this, besides many other questions, troubled him, and were perpetually beating about his brain, and he reached Rome fagged and worn out, both in mind and body. Yet still he scarcely allowed himself rest—did not rest, until he stood by the bedside of his dying friend.

Yes, Fred Stanhope was dying; dying from the effects of a fall from his horse at the early age of thirty-four; so young, yet in the midst of a dissipated, wasted life. All this came with a sudden shock upon Raymond. All this the burnt letter would have told him, as also that his friend, with whom he had quarelled three years ago, acknowledged his error, and begged to see him, to hold his hand in friendship once more before he died.

Mrs. Stanhope watched beside her son, and welcomed Raymond gratefully.

" He has been asking for you all day," she said, " until a sudden change set in about an hour ago; since which his brain has been wandering, and I fear he will not recognise you. We felt sure you would come ; at least I did, although I did not expect you so soon."

" I have travelled night and day," he answered but did not say his journey concerned another beside his dying friend. This would have led to a confession he wished to avoid.

His friend's state was a misadventure Mr. Bedfield had not calculated upon, when he promised his cousin to be absent if possible only a week. This was not only, not possible—but an impossibility. How ! now he had come so far ; leave the dying man before he was conscious of his presence ? How go away in the face of that sorrowing mother, who hailed his presence as the one boon her son craved for ? No, though consumed with more harassing thoughts than when he journeyed to Rome, he must wait—wait.

Each day saw him at the post office—that duty was not entrusted to Jackson—and each day saw him disappointed. But on the third, there was a letter, yet his spirits sank when he found it had not the Broadbelt postmark. If the chaperon would only go away quietly and without fuss,. and save him all further trouble? So he thought as he journeyed homewards, opened his letter, and read it.

"I have left as you wished. Is not your will law? I am here in Paris. Once more thrown by your act on the world without money or friends. You have hunted me to the earth. Do you feel how bitterly you have punished me? Does your heart feel regret or remorse for your work now? It is your work you know. Do you think to-night or for many nights to come, you will sleep on your pillow any the easier for it? I am miserable and alone in this wretched lodging. My money all gone, or nearly so. Surely even your enmity cannot wish me worse, or allow me to starve.

"M. C."

"Hurrah!" shouted Mr. Bedfield, "earthed at last! And I am glad of it; she deserves all I have done and something worse."

But presently feelings of compunction arose.

"Poor devil!" he said, "She is as clever a woman as I ever saw, and deserves a better fate. Perhaps she is not quite so black as my imagination paints her. As to my will being law that's all rubbish! I won't starve her out. I'll be generous and merciful. She deserves it for giving up the siege so quietly."

Before he returned to his friend's hotel, he wrote to the address she gave, a small street in the suburb of Saint Antoine, and enclosed her a cheque for twenty pounds.

Then once more he betook himself to Fred Stanhope, with at least, on one subject, an easier and a lighter heart.

"Do not go in," said Mrs. Stanhope, as he laid his hand on the handle of the bed-room door, "don't go in. He is better and asleep. God grant the change may not be a deceiving one. The physicians say the chances are, he will be himself again when he wakes."

They were right. He was better. And again

better still a few days after, and moved by his own express desire on to the sofa in his mother's sitting-room.

Mrs. Stanhope was sanguine—very sanguine now, but the physicians still looked grave. There was no cheering, hopeful look on their faces.

Raymond Bedfield's days were almost entirely devoted to his friend; there was no ill feeling on the mind of either; all that was past, and perhaps forgotten.

One morning he found him in a half reclining posture, leaning over a paper he had but just folded up and directed.

"Is this allowable, Fred? or is it not rather very imprudent?"

"I did not think *you* were deceived, Raymond. I am not."

"As how?"

"I am dying, old fellow, dying as fast and sure, and as steadily, as that winter's sun will set ere the evening closes in. Don't you be deceived as well as my mother. It is but a flickering of the candle before it goes out. I have not many days left now ; you may shake your head, but it is so ; and—and there is one thought haunts me, troubles me, Raymond ; did trouble me even before I came to this pass. Can you guess it ?"

" I—that is—no."

" It's that girl, Raymond."

" Don't let that trouble you, Fred."

" But I must. I do," said he, excitedly. " That's what I have been writing about," and he laid his hand on the paper beside him. " I behaved badly to her, Raymond ; I did not think so then, but I think so now. That old hag, her mother, regularly enmeshed me. She would have sold her own soul for gold, and why not her daughter's ? But I don't accuse her to excuse my own sin, which God knows was bad enough. But—but, Raymond, she must not starve. I have written all my wishes here, and you will see to them, old fellow, won't you ? You'll find her out after I'm gone ? You'll do that for me ?"

" I will," answered Mr. Bedfield.

"That's a good fellow. I could not rest quiet in my grave if I thought you wouldn't. I have never forgotten her, Raymond, though I thought I had; but it's all come upon me again since I have been lying here. She may be steeped in sin and guilt."

"She may be dead."

"I think not. I know she was not a year ago. She was fond of life; a very coward where that was threatened. You will hunt her up for me, as I wish I could do. You will tell her how I thought of her at the last. You will give her the letter you will find in that parcel, and say that one of my last wishes was for her happiness. You will do all this?"

"I will."

"You promise me?"

"I swear it most solemnly."

"I am content. I shall die all the happier, Raymond. She was proud. She would never accept a farthing from me in life, poor girl. But in death it will be different. You will per-

suade her—if need be, Raymond—persuade her
for my sake; but say not a word—a whisper—if
she be married, and happy. It's all written down
on that paper.   My mother will give the money
for my sake.   I think there is very little my
mother would not do for me."

"Don't only think it, Fred," said Mrs. Stanhope, who had entered at the moment; "be sure
of it."

"It's only a—a last wish, mother," said Mr.
Stanhope, fearful of grieving her, and hesitating
at reminding her of what he knew she did not
believe, or rather flattered herself would not
be.

"And therefore a more binding one," she an-
wered.   "I will promise it whatever it is."

"Blind to my sins and follies even yet,
mother.   What an undutiful son I have been!
Can you forgive me?"

"Hush!" she said, stooping over him and
wiping the damp moisture from his brow, and
kissing him fondly.   "Hush! I have nothing to

forgive.   You have ever been a dutiful son to me."

"God bless you, dear mother."

" I do not think Fred looks so well," said Mrs. Stanhope, as she wished Raymond good-bye, " or else the bright fresh faces I met out walking have made me think his looks pale in comparison."

Mr. Bedfield fidgetted for a letter from the chaperon.   No answer had come to his remittance, although he had requested one.   Suppose she had hoaxed him, and not left Stonycleft after all ?   But at the end of a week of impatience and worry, he received one in the same scrawly hand as before, and which he thought, beat even poor Fred's, in the difficulty of deciphering.   It was not so much an unladylike hand, as it was an— as he termed it—execrable one.

" Thank you for the money.   How can I thank you enough !   A pound a year for twenty years !
What beggar could expect more ? Twenty pounds from you is indeed a princely, munificent gift;

and I think of it as such as I lay here, worn out and ill—*earthed* as you would call it. Yes, I am ill; ill in mind and body. And yet I give my grateful thanks to you, who have struck the blow, and made me as I am, friendless and ill. You have my grateful thanks, and deserve them; may you be rewarded some day for it. You will be, and in a manner you least expect.

"M. C."

No, Raymond did not relish the letter at all. He crushed it up in his hand snappishly with a growl of dissatisfaction, as he walked off to bed.

Within the next few days Mr. Stanhope grew worse. It had been but a flickering of the candle as he had said. It had burnt up brightly for a time, and then was gone almost suddenly. His mother, who sat beside him, scarce knew when he was dead.

But Raymond, felt a slight pressure of the hand he held. Leaning over him, he caught the word "Remember!" and yet another, which sounded like a woman's name, came faintly—very faintly from his lips; and he was at rest—at rest for evermore, from all the troubles and cares, the sins and follies of this world.

Again Mr. Bedfield journeyed—journeyed homewards.

They travelled together; himself and that sorrowing, bereaved mother, until they reached Paris. Here they separated. She for her solitary home in England; he to remain. But he had a motive for this delay, though all his thoughts and wishes were turning and flying constantly, and ever in the direction of Stonycleft. Why was it so? Ah! that he never paused to consider, but see the chaperon once more he would. It was a miserable quarter this street she lived in, but he found it, nevertheless. How would she receive him? And would she receive him? or would she refuse? And was she ill, or was she only shamming? Perhaps his heart did smite him with a twinge of compunction as he walked down the wretched street, and his eye fell upon the dirty, slip-shod girl, who opened the door.

" Mamselle Castelle," said she, as he made known his demand. " Ah, *cette pauvre Mamselle* was very ill—very. Impossible Monsieur could see her. Was he her brother or her lover? But all the same, *Mamselle* was too ill to see him. No, she did not know whát was the matter, but *Mamselle* cried *beaucoup* all day; and ah! *mon Dieu!* how she moaned at night! .Pauline could not sleep for pity. Did a docter see her. Ah! yes! M. Duvoisin, who lived *Numero sept*, the *Rue Lamartine.*"

His conscience pricked uncomfortably by all he had heard, Raymond bent his steps to *Monsieur le docteur's.*

He was at home that man of physic, with his spectacles and moustaches, his compliments and grimaces, and his wiry, spider-like body; and " would be happy, very happy to give—M. Castelle ?"— here an interrogative bow and grimace, which Mr. Bedfield did not contradict,—

" Mademoiselle's brother,"—another grimace,—
all the information in his power. She was very
ill, this *pauvre demoiselle;* ill not so much in
body as mind. She was always fretting, and to-
day her head was hot, and her pulse quick, had
every symptom of fever, etc. Was M. Castelle
going to remain? No. Would M. Castelle be
pleased to give M Duvoisin his address in Paris?"

No, Mr. Bedfield would not even do that, could
not, as he was going that very evening to England; but he gave him a ten pound note to cover
any expenses he might deem necessary for his
patient, as also his solicitor's address, in case she
should be worse, when he was to be sent for immediately, even telegraphed for, if need be.

They parted mutually satisfied, the doctor
overwhelming him with bows and grimaces,
and a succession of " *bon voyage.*"

Home! Home, once more! What mattered
how the wind blew, or how rough and boisterous
the chopping seas of the Channel; they bore him
home to dear old England, to Stonycleft, and to

Cynthia. Yes, Raymond Bedfield was going to Stonycleft, although six weeks and more had dragged wearily by, since he had left it so hurriedly under the promise of returning as hastily.

Would his cousin be glad to see him ? Would his uncle forget their last mortifying conversation, and welcome him. How had the chaperon left, and what excuse had she made for going so suddenly ? How had she looked, and what had she said ? He flattered himself that triumphing over a fallen enemy had nothing to do with all this. It was not the pleasure of placing his foot on the neck of the vanquished, but curiosity, mere idle curiosity.

The snow covered the ground thickly, was covering it still, as Mr. Bedfield drove up to the park gates in the gig he had hired at the Station Inn, thinking it would bear him along quicker than a fly. But the horse was a sorry one, and the ground heavy.

" How are they all at the house ?" he asked of the man at the Lodge.

But the man was a little deaf, and had not evidently heard aright.

" Just been home a week, sir," he replied.

Strange ! Where had they been ? But he would learn soon enough, he thought. He got on but slowly. The evening had set in, and the darkness increased, while the driving snow and sleet beat full in his face, and almost blinded him. He was obliged to go, at—to him, in his impatience—a snail's pace.

" Have they sat down to dinner?" he asked, as he shook the snow off his coat, and prepared to enter the hall.

" No, sir ; the ladies have but just gone into the drawing-room."

Ladies ! There were visitors, then. But there was no help for it; and with a hasty brush and wash, he was on his way downstairs again.

" Mr. Bedfield," vociferated a man-servant, like a clap of thunder in his ear, as he threw open the door of the drawing-room.

There were two ladies in the room. His cousin

Cynthia, who started forward, and welcomed him
with a half-smothered cry and reproachful look;
and another, whose back was turned to him, as
she stood before the fire; her tall, well-made
figure looking almost queen-like, in the heavy,
rich folds of a black velvet dress, which swept
proudly around her form, floating away in the
distance on the ground behind her. A chain of
pearls, as white as the snow flakes without, bound
her small, fair white throat, her arms, and wound
in and out the masses of her magnificent raven
hair.

Mr. Bedfield could see the shadow of her face
in the glass as she stood. In another moment
she turned and faced him.

It was the chaperon ! regally dressed, and
wonderfully handsome ; but the chaperon still.

The room reeled before Raymond Bedfield's
eyes; he steadied himself by the table. One
moment ! Then he spoke :

" Serpent ! Deceiver !" he exclaimed; " I
have unmasked you. You are—" he drew close

—closer still, while he almost hissed some words into her ear.

" Hush! Hush!" whispered Cynthia, springing to his side. " You are too late. Hush!—papa!"

As she spoke Sir Cyrus entered.

He looked at his nephew's white, excited face; and then at the chaperon, whose very lips were paling, and went over and stood by her side, as though protecting her—defying him.

"My wife! Lady Bedfield!" he said, in a loud ; decided ; care-nought voice.

But Lady Bedfield had fainted ere the words had hardly passed his lips, and lay partly on the ground, partly supported by the chair behind her, while the rich black velvet dress fell like a pall about and around her.

END OF VOL. I.

T. C. Newby, 30. Welbeck Street, Cavendish Square, London.